The Lighthouse Keeper's Lass

EMMA HARDWICK

Drina

ROMANCE
PUBLISHING

COPYRIGHT

CONTENTS

1

THE UNWANTED CHILD

One Sunday, twelve-year-old Isla was balancing precariously on a rickety wooden stool and hanging washing on a line that stretched from the weathered back door to the fence behind the cottage. The wind was blowing a gale but the air was dry, and there was no indication of rain.

For Isla, this Sunday was no different to any other. Her mother, Freya, had sent her to collect wood for the fire and then ordered her to the pump to fill the buckets with water. Isla had spent the morning washing the cottage floors, kneeling on the rough stones until her knees were grazed. Next was the laundry. Freya would hoard all of the dirty clothes for a Sunday, then she would palm the washing off on her daughter.

Thankfully it was summer because they were hellish tasks in the freezing winter. The poor unloved lass would be forced to endure them with chilblained hands that bled as she scrubbed and stung in the water.

"Get on with it," shouted her mother. "There is no promising when the rain will move in."

Freya Dickson had an endless array of chores for Isla, and it didn't matter that it was the Lord's Day. On Sundays, most families would be at church or resting, it was the only day that the pits were closed, and the exhausted miners could enjoy a day above ground. For Freya, it was all balderdash, and she had no intention of ever seeing the inside of a church for as long as she lived - or after her death.

"I am warning you, Isla, you have tasted the tip of the whip more than once because you are a lazy little troll, so get cracking if you want to avoid another beating," the bitter woman roared. Freya Dickson spat out her child's name like it was poison on her tongue.

"I've had to strike you with briar how many times to teach you a lesson? Still, you do not listen, you disobedient little witch. Lift up that dress," Freya ordered.

Isla ignored her.

"I told yer to lift it!"

Freya walked towards Isla menacingly. She watched Isla struggle to balance on the stool, and it thrilled the cold-hearted woman to witness her discomfort. Isla's eyes showed no emotion.

Freya wouldn't be content until she had shamed the girl and driven fear into her heart. These days, however, Isla was becoming more stoic and difficult to intimidate. When the child was young, Freya fed off the terror she saw on the little girl's face. Now she only had two weapons to use against the child. One was pain and the other, humiliation.

Isla lifted the dirty skirt and revealed her legs to her mother.

> "Can you see those marks? That was from last
> week's beating. There will be more where that
> came from."

Isla's legs were a crisscross of lines and bloody scabs where the thorns on the briars had ripped her skin.

Isla lowered her dress. Her lips were quivering, and her eyes were filled with tears. No longer a child, she was a girl on the edge of womanhood. She glared at her mother's back, wishing her to die soon. It wasn't the first time she had cursed Freya Dickson to die. Alas, God didn't hear her pleas because Freya continued to rise from her bed, day in and day out. Isla prayed relentlessly. She knew that one day God would have time to fulfil her request. Sometimes, Isla was convinced that her mother had made a deal with the devil to live forever.

> "Your father is not here to protect you," shouted
> Freya, who was working herself into a frenzy
> which always ended in Isla being beaten.

> "Ma, what else must I do for you?" Isla asked
> Freya, trying to change the subject.

> "Get into that barn."

Freya pointed at a small tumbledown structure that housed a cow and a few scrawny hens.

> "I want all that dung cleaned up and dug into the
> garden by nightfall."

It was a colossal job for so late in the day, and without doubt, Isla would still be digging the manure into the vegetable garden after dark. Rather than get angry, she rejoiced as her mother stomped back towards their home. It didn't save Isla from her lot, but it ensured that she wouldn't have the woman tormenting her for the whole afternoon. Isla set to work, the shovel scraping against the cold stony floor of the tiny barn.

Back in the cottage, Freya would drink her beloved gin until she collapsed on the rusted steel cot that she slept on. She would remain that way until the early hours of the morning when she would get up and finish what was left in the bottle. She would only wake up late the following day. By that time, Isla would already be at school, the only place where she was safe from her harpy of a mother.

2

FREYA

Freya Dickson was the product of a violent past, extreme cruelty, and abuse. She was in her late thirties, but looking at her, you would never have guessed it. She was emaciated, and her sinewy limbs looked like a dying oak tree's twisted, tortured branches. Her yellowy skin was stretched over her face like vellum, which gave her a likeness to the ancient mummies of antiquity. You could see her skull through her thinning hair. Her teeth were the same colour as her skin, and there were many missing. She gave the frightening impression of being an ancient relic, spiteful, all-knowing, and malevolent.

Freya had grown up in Callington, on the eastern edge of Bodmin Moor. Her father was a copper miner, or rather, a highly qualified engineer that designed the heavy machinery used on the mine. Of German stock, Rudolph Wagner was a gentle, exhausted man who simply plodded through life doing just enough to get by. He had no ambition and always followed the path of least resistance. It was no surprise that this attitude had contributed to 'Old Rudy's' survival as he had reached his sixties when few miners survived beyond forty. The meek man had provided well for his family, and they lived in an immaculate six-roomed cottage with a beautiful garden. It was one of the finest houses in the impoverished town of Callington.

Rudy married his sweetheart when he was twenty, and she was just sixteen. Gwen Wagner was as gentle as Rudy, and they settled into a peaceful, predictable life. Gwen was the homemaker, gifted in making every penny stretch without the family feeling hard done by. Within five years, Gwen had given birth to three strapping, blonde-haired, blue-eyed sons. Although Karl, Stefan and Klaus were well-loved, they were not well-raised. Other children of Germanic ancestry had excellent manners, but Rudy was a reluctant disciplinarian. Gwen was easily overwhelmed by her three wily boys. They were gifted with the subtle, yet powerful art of manipulation.

Gwen didn't have another child for ten years, and she was surprised that she fell pregnant because the passion between her and Rudy had long-since waned. They were still in love, but by the time they put their heads on the pillow at night, they only wanted to sleep. When Rudy was working the night shift, it was worse. They hardly saw each other at all. Little Freya was born in the spring. Rudy and Gwen were elated. They had been given a wonderful gift that brought them so much joy, and the little girl became the centre of their lives.

Karl, Stefan and Klaus were already developing a reputation for being hooligans. The church and school continually wrote letters to Rudy and Gwen complaining of their behaviour. Rudy chastised them, and Gwen was embarrassed, but neither one had the mettle to take a rod to them. At school, they were abrupt and disrespectful. They were suspected of vandalising the local churchyard. A police constable had called on the Wagners and warned them that the youths would be gaoled if they were caught perpetrating any criminal act. Even though they no longer had a civic outlet for their hidden fury, and it was more a decision than a consequence that the three brothers began tormenting their baby sister.

Somehow, the four Wagner children had inherited a cold, vindictive streak. Rudy and Gwen didn't know where they had gone wrong in raising them and constantly berated themselves for being bad parents. Gwen spent many days in tears. She found it difficult controlling her three sons and pacifying an ever-screaming baby. When they were not persecuting Freya, the three Wagner boys were warring amongst themselves, only to rally around each other when one was threatened by Gwen or Rudy trying 'one last time' to pull them back into line.

Rudy realised that Gwen was at the end of her tether. He suggested she find a housekeeper to take some pressure off, and Gwen didn't hesitate in accepting the offer. Angeline Murray was a ruddy woman from the far north. Gwen had chosen her for her forthright attitude, convinced that the woman was sufficiently resilient to tolerate the boys' behaviour. Within a month, Mrs Murray identified the cause of Freya's unhappiness. Gwen had asked her to bathe the little girl, and when she removed Freya's clothes, she was horrified to see the sores and bruises on her little body. She also noted that every time Freya was left alone with her brothers, it wouldn't be long before she was screaming and unhappy. Mrs Murray put two and two together and then presented Freya's case to her parents. Mrs Murray was disgusted with Gwen. Surely, she must have seen the damage when she bathed her child. What mother would allow this to happen?

Rudy and Gwen summoned Karl, Stefan and Klaus to the parlour. They confronted their sons while Mrs Murray watched the proceedings. The outcome was moot. There were denials, accusations, and they took the liberty of confronting Mrs Murray in front of their parents. Rudy and Gwen did nothing to control the situation. They just wished it would end.

In defence of Gwen, she watched Freya more closely, refusing to leave Freya alone with her brothers. There was a distinct change in the child's mood. Within a month, Mrs Murray broke her arm. She had stepped on a few marbles that someone accidentally left on the staircase. Over the coming years, Gwen would employ a steady stream of feisty but accident-prone housekeepers. Finally, her sons left home, and all the bad luck ended.

Until then however, Freya continued to suffer at the hands of her brothers, and a particularly dreadful incident continued to plague her thoughts.

One night, when her exhausted parents had retired, the brothers returned home late from the pub, very much worse for wear. They tumbled through the door, hunting through all the cupboards for more to drink. Freya came to see what the racket was, and immediately, they began abusing her, first with words, then with slaps and shoves.

"Leave me alone, or you'll regret it," Freya
protested, hoping it didn't sound like an empty
threat.

Incensed and intoxicated, Klaus grabbed her by the shoulders, frog-marched her outside, and pushed her out into the dark and uneven lane. Tripping over her long skirt, she landed on the gritty cobbles with a heavy thud. Klaus snarled like a rottweiler sensing blood.

"Stop it, Klaus. Stop."

The words achieved nothing. As a terrified Freya looked on, Klaus unbuckled his heavy leather belt. It slipped almost silently through its loops. He raised his right arm high above his contorted face and whipped the strap down. The two other brothers smirked at her with icy cold eyes. Despite the excruciating lash, Freya succeeded in catching hold of the belt and tugged it with all her might. Klaus, slowed with drink and now off-balance toppled forwards. He clambered onto all-fours, then seized his sister by her slender throat and held her until the skin broke and the blood flowed.

"Hey," called out a voice in the darkness. "You there. Leave that woman alone!"

A piercing police whistle permeated the air. Stefan and Karl slipped away from the dark doorway and into the safety of the house as Constable Barraclough marched up to the sprawling siblings, fully intending to arrest the attacker. When he saw it was Klaus Wagner he flinched and thought it better to give a stern warning instead.

When her brothers fled the nest, it was the only time of her life that Freya got close to being happy. She and her mother spent hours together. The peace was sublime, and soon, Gwen didn't miss her sons. Word had it that the three of them were entering into one dodgy scheme after the other, but their beleaguered mother buried her head in the sand.

In her mind, they were men, they were out of her house, and she never wanted to see them again.

Gwen did feel sorry for Rudy, though. While she hid away at the house, he bore the brunt of the embarrassment. Her hard-working husband had fathered three 'ne'er do wells', and he was often ridiculed, or worse, confronted because of it. After a while, Rudy stopped going out, unable to bear the torment any more. He and Gwen became more reclusive and had few friends.

Freya developed into a plain girl. At fifteen, she was small and appeared to be frail. She was pale with mousy brown hair and had small, delicate facial features. Her eyes were dim and watery. Anyone who took the time to look into the almost colourless orbs would easily identify the underlying coldness. She was easily belittled by her peers as she seemed slow. Granted, she was different, but people made a great mistake thinking that she was stupid.

Freya was observant and cunning. She had to be, given that she grew up having to outwit her brothers or suffer their cruelty.

3

KLAUS, STEFAN, AND KARL

Klaus, Stefan, and Karl had become notorious for their underhanded activities. To date, the police had never been able to gather sufficient evidence or witnesses to testify against the brothers. Rudy could no longer bear people whispering behind their hands every time he walked down the street. After years of degradation, Rudy finally told Gwen that he was retiring from his position at the local mine and that he had saved enough money to move them to one of the smaller villages further along the coast.

"It's a tiny place. No one will know us," he trilled,
his excited eyes staring deeply into hers.

Gwen embraced the bold decision, and, despite the tremendous upheaval, even Freya was relieved they were leaving the busybodies, gossips, and an endless stream of furious townsfolk. The brothers' reign of terror was finally losing its grip on them.

The move to the ideal spot was not going to be easy. A few weeks earlier when Rudy first mulled over his options, he discovered that his sons were now living on the Cornish north coast. There were constant rumours of them being seen in the town of St Ives, and that they had purchased several fishing boats. More sightings followed at many of the little coves and quays that dotted the north shore.

At first, he hoped that they had decided to earn an honest living, but he soon came to his senses and shelved his plan to go to St Ives. He didn't want to be anywhere near the three criminals he had fathered, and so instead, he chose to move the family to Polperro, a tiny coastal village miles away to the south.

The Wagners were well accepted in their new community. The locals soon learnt that Rudy was an engineer and began to approach him for advice. He could go into the pubs and taverns without fear of embarrassment, and his new life began. Even when word did reach the village that he was the father of the notorious Wagner boys on the north coast, nobody treated him, Gwen or Freya, differently. The family were grateful Rudy's skills were of value to others, and he was a likeable fellow.

Freya chose to keep to herself. Thankfully, her school years were over, and she didn't have to suffer the trepidation of meeting a multitude of new people. No matter how hard people tried to reach out to her, Freya would always feel like the outsider, standing alone, looking in.

The young woman spent hours walking on the beach, and she was content to be isolated. It also gave her time to think. Sadly, they were often dark thoughts. She was still filled with bitterness towards Karl, Stefan, and Klaus. Pacing along the shoreline she vowed that one day, when they least expected it, she would strike back for all she had suffered at their hands. The hatred was deep-seated. It made her fearless and impatient to act, which in turn made her vulnerable to a nasty planned surprise.

*

The trouble between the feuding siblings worsened on New Year's Eve, just before dawn. That morning, Freya watched as three boats sailed into Polperro harbour, unaware of the significance of their appearance.

After the family's move, Freya had developed a daily ritual of getting up before sunrise, walking to the small quayside, and watching the day begin. As soon as light appeared on the horizon, she would walk to the fish market where she'd found a job. The old woman who took her on taught her how to clean and gut fish, and the razor-sharp knife slicing through the white flesh gave Freya a curiously instinctive sense of satisfaction. She felt comfortable and secure with it in her hand, and she decided to buy one to keep on her person. Freya went to the tiny hardware shop and bought a penknife. A few days later, she observed how the fish wives sharpened their blades using an oilstone, so she bought one of those too.

Retiring to her room at night, she spent hours honing the blade, and was only satisfied when, with only the faintest touch, she could draw blood from her finger. Not even Freya knew why she wanted the small weapon. All she knew was that it completed her.

That evening, not wanting to join in the festivities, Freya went for a stroll, despite the awful weather. The clouds hung low and thick over the coastline, blocking the light of the moon. The cold air was dense and still. The sea was as smooth as a lake, and only the tiniest of waves broke against the shore. The only sound that could be heard coming out of the blackness was that of the boat oars that gently dipped into the water. Anyone passing by would easily mistake it for water casually lapping up against the wooden bows of fishing boats sheltering in the quay.

Freya was invisible in the shadows of the harbour wall, and the men didn't know that she was there. Peering into the gloom, the ships became clearer as they approached. She assumed there must have been a considerable amount of cargo stowed on the boats because there were approximately ten crewmen in each one. She watched while they offloaded the heavy crates in silence. A horse-drawn cart appeared and collected the boxes, and when it was fully loaded, it trundled off and disappeared into the night.

Then, three men walked past where she was hiding, and she held her breath. They were talking to each other in low voices, and although she didn't see their faces, she recognised their tone. They were the voices of her brothers. Freya was taken off guard and panicked, a terrified cornered animal. All she wanted to do was escape from the harbour, escape from them. If she'd only stayed where she was, she would have been safe.

Freya edged herself along the wall, feeling her way as she went along. When she reached the cobbled unloading area, however, she was totally exposed. She panicked knowing the men could see her vague silhouette. Petrified, she stumbled but righted herself and began to run. She'd not considered that her brothers would have lookouts scouring the quayside. Freya didn't get the opportunity to escape. As she turned to run, she felt two powerful arms seize her, and then one calloused, stinking hand covered her mouth. Freya fought and kicked to get away, but it was futile. The man didn't speak to her, but he put his hand around her throat and squeezed. It was a warning.

*

Klaus, Stefan, and Karl returned to the boats and prepared to leave. They had to be clear of the harbour before daylight flooded the heavens. They watched their man approach the boat, carrying a bundle. As the fellow got closer, they saw that it was a person.

The giant of a man threw Freya down at her brothers' feet, knocking the wind out of her. She was wet and dirty, and her dress was torn.

"What is this, Samson?" Klaus whispered harshly, nudging the pile at his feet with the toe of his hob-nailed boot.

"Found her spying, captain," answered the mountain of a man.

Klaus bent over, grabbed Freya by her hair, and pulled her to her feet. He looked at her face and frowned.

"You!"

Klaus tightened his grip on her locks and she winced, angling her head for his brothers to inspect. Stefan and Karl stepped forward in the foggy air and took a good look at the woman.

"How the devil did she get here?" Stefan snarled.

"Get rid of her," said Karl.

Klaus shoved her towards the large man.

"She's yours. You can have her. Make it fast and
kill her when you're finished."

Nothing that Freya did was premeditated. It was an act of
desperation. She put her hand in her pocket and pulled out
the penknife, and expertly flipped it open. No one saw it
with no sunlight to reflect off the blade.

Smirking then licking his lips, Samson put out his hands to
grab her chest. She lunged at him. Instinctively, he tried to
catch her hand but caught the invisible blade instead. The
knife was so sharp that it took him a few seconds to realise
that he was injured. He pulled his hand towards his face and
yelped. When he felt the warm blood running down his
arm, he went into a frenzy and tried to attack her again.
This time, the blade plunged into his inner thigh. It sliced
through the muscle effortlessly and hit an artery. Warm
sticky blood began to seep from the wound and soaked
through his trousers. The sun finally began to penetrate
through the low cloud and mist, revealing the full horror of
the scene. Freya froze.

"We can't leave him here, they'll have us for
murder!" muttered Karl in a panic.

"Load him in the boat," ordered Stefan.

"Then what will we do with him?" Karl asked.

"We'll dump him at sea. No one will ever find him. These blokes better keep their mouths tightly shut, or they will be done for," Klaus said, looking round at his crew menacingly..

The three brothers angrily fought off the deluded crewmen trying to treat Samson's gaping leg wound. The perverted monster was already dead. The shale on the beach was drenched with blood that would only be washed away at high tide.

"Put Freya in the boat as well," said Karl.

The crew on the sailing boats were ordinary fishermen with families. Of course, all of them did a bit of smuggling to *'get them through tough times'*, but what they saw on the beach was shocking. Smuggling was supposed to be an adventure, but now it had resulted in a murder. It would only be a matter of time before someone learned about it, and they would all be culpable by way of their silence.

The Wagner men feared that they had lost a good crew. Surely, they would all want to distance themselves from the killing to save their own skins. The brothers didn't know how they were going to contain the knowledge of the event. They certainly couldn't murder thirty men at once, could they?

Klaus, Stefan and Karl turned around but Freya was gone. Their heads spun round like millstones, desperate to catch a glimpse of her. Finally, they saw her dark, nimble figure scaling the harbour wall. They tried to follow but were too slow. Now, they were betwixt and between. She knew their secret, and they were going to have to kill her—just not now.

*

As the sun rose, an intense red strip formed along the horizon. On deck, a mournful Stefan assessed the situation. In silence, Klaus and Karl bristled with fury.

> "We have no choice but to let her go, this time. We can't hang around the harbour with this on board," he warned, staring at Samson's corpse. "Even with him gone, our fishing boats have no nets, so it's obvious something's not right. We're in grave danger of the coppers giving our collars a feel. And, I don't know about you fellows but I'm determined not to spend the rest of my life in gaol for smuggling—or swinging for murder."

His siblings sprang into action.

> "Right, you men, time to set sail," barked Karl, before he and Klaus leapt onto their own boats. "Anchors aweigh!"

The rigging creaked as the three ships began to turn. If there had been oars, the brothers would have flogged the men to row faster, as if they were Roman galley slaves.

After a tense few minutes, the boats rounded the cliff heads just before the first fishermen arrived at Polperro harbour, but the escape was too close for comfort, and the crew were livid. The men quietly decided that would be their last trip with the brothers—whether for fishing or more nefarious activities.

*

Freya fled the quay with the bloody knife still in her hand, relieved that the foggy streets were deserted and no one noticed. The small, prettily painted shops that lined the waterfront went past in a blur until she turned left into the gloomy narrow lane that led to her home. The house was at the top of a steep hill, but that didn't slow her down. Her legs were aching from the climb, and she couldn't catch her breath. The steps to the front entrance were taken two at a time. Freya, desperate to collapse in a heap, grabbed the door handle with her left hand, twisted it awkwardly, then leant against the heavy oak door until it gave way. Dashing along the hallway, she went straight towards the kitchen, knowing her parents would be there at the table drinking their morning tea.

Freya reached the doorway and stopped abruptly. She wanted to speak, but she couldn't. Her body wasn't cooperating. Temporarily confused, Rudy and Gwen stared at their dishevelled daughter who appeared in the doorway like a ghoul. They hardly recognised the girl who stood in front of them with her dress bloodstained and a small sticky knife in her hand. Her hair was wilder, and she was sodden with sweat. With eyes wide and glassy, her mind seemed attuned to the smallest movements and finest sounds in the house. Her brain had taken over her body like an automaton designed to survive. The machine in her head was on high alert, and it was determined to protect Freya, its fragile host.

"What have you done?" Gwen screamed in horror.

Freya, ice-cold and beginning to tremble, was unable to answer her mother. She couldn't get enough air and was gulping like a suffocating fish lying at the bottom of a boat.

"Damn it, child!" cursed the usually passive Rudy. "Answer your mother, or must I beat the truth out of you?"

Standing up, he raised his arm readying himself to hit her. It was the first time ever that Rudy had threatened Freya. He had never even reprimanded his wayward sons this aggressively. The poor girl gasped for breath and tried to speak, but she could only get out a few words.

"Klaus," she stammered. "He wants to murder me."

"That's impossible, Freya. They are up at St Ives, nowhere near here," Gwen told her.

"All three of them were in the harbour before dawn. They were smuggling," Freya panted defiantly. "I saw the booty being unloaded. Lots of it. I must tell the police what happened."

"Hush your mouth!" her mother yelled at her. "Not a word about smuggling and police. Do you hear me?"

"Perhaps you are the one the police should be interested in?" Rudy bellowed. "You're already guilty of something, holding that knife, covered with blood."

"I was defending myself," protested Freya, finally controlling her breathing.

"You cannot blame this on your brothers," shouted her mother, attempting to hide her dread. "Yes, they are bad men. But they would never try to murder you."

"Enough!" Freya snapped, using the last of her energy to defend herself. "This is what happened throughout my childhood. My brothers would terrorise me, and you end up condoning their violent behaviour because of your inaction. I can't stand the sight of you. In fact, I hate you!"

They had finally broken her. Her body crumpled as she slid down onto a chair by the kitchen door. Feeling rejected, her head dropped as she slumped, and soon she resembled a little sack of abandoned bones. She dropped her chin onto her chest and began to cry. The sound came from deep within her body, and it terrified her parents. Rudy knew that the day would be a watershed for Freya, she would either find a way to survive it, or it would ruin her forever.

Maternal instinct took over and Gwen grabbed her daughter's hand and pulled her from the kitchen. She shoved the girl into the icy-cold annexe where they did the laundry and swung the door closed.

"Take everything off." she yelled at the stunned little figure. "Now!"

Gwen saw the marks around Freya's throat and bruises all over her body, but she ignored them. The beleaguered mother had just begun to forge a new, happier life in Polperro, and now that was in jeopardy. These days, she and her husband lived a quiet life. They had made friends, and they could walk down a street with their heads held high. Everyone knew that their sons were horrid men, but so far, the locals were unaware of the connection.

She gathered up Freya's blood-stained clothes, picked up the shoes and the knife then disappeared back into the kitchen. Freya heard her mother push her belongings into the belly of the large cast-iron stove while her father watched in silence. Then, she overheard her mother's poisonous whispering wafting through the gap in the door.

> "Rudy, I am tired of our treacherous children, including Freya. I could cope with her always being miserable. But this latest debacle?" she complained, before falling silent for a moment. "—They were all a disappointment to me, and I wish that I'd never had them."

Gwen went back into the annexe and handed Freya some clean clothes. As she watched her daughter get dressed, rage overcame her and she grabbed the naked girl by the arm then shoved her against the wall. Nose-to-nose, she looked into Freya's face, which had suddenly become so ugly to her. It was the first and last time that Gwen would feel hatred. She shoved her finger under her daughter's nose violently and said the words that would destroy Freya's fragile mind completely.

"You are as evil as your brothers. I hate you. I want you out of my house today. Never ever come back here. I never want to see you for as long as I live."

Later, when she'd calmed down, Gwen regretted her words, but the damage was absolute. Gwen, Rudy, and Freya would never reconcile.

4

METAMORPHOSIS

Freya was late for work that day and it made Mrs Landon, the fishwife, furious with her. For two long hours, the old woman stooped over a barrel, with the gruesome task of gutting and cleaning fish. She used the time to plan how she would give the ungrateful, unreliable girl the sack.

"There are plenty of young women looking for work," she muttered. "I'll have a new girl to replace Freya by midday."

Thrusting her fingers into the silvery fish's red belly, she gave a tug on the entrails to release them from the base of the head. The whole lot was tossed into a bucket. Next to go was the liver, deftly scraped away from the backbone.

"It is a pity that Freya has to go. She was an excellent, if strange, worker. Never really given me a day of bother. Still, I won't tolerate laziness even if it is New Year's Eve."

Mrs Landon slashed out the gills of the last fish in the barrel, then slammed her knife down on the table. Her tired hands were throbbing. Until now, she'd not realised how fast her underling worked. She desperately needed a cup of tea and put a kettle of water on the fire. When she looked up, Freya was standing in front of her, carrying a carpet bag. Freya couldn't look Mrs Landon in the eye. The girl knew that the fishwife would be livid about her tardiness and that she would likely lose her job because of her wretched brothers, and there was nothing she could do about it. Worse, she didn't think honesty would help her plight. If her story was so far-fetched that not even her parents would accept it as truth, how would it sound to a stranger? She lamented how furious Mrs Landon seemed as she walked over. Alone and abandoned, Freya's despair grew, as she dropped the bag and her bottom lip trembled. Dressed strangely, in tattered, ill-fitting clothes, she looked a state.

*

All Mrs Landon's anger left her when she saw the state that the girl was in.

"Oh, lass, what has happened to you?"

Freya was as pale as a ghost, even though her puffy eyes were pinkish, and her cold, reddened nose was running. It was obvious to Mrs Landon that she'd been crying. It wasn't just her appearance that hinted there was something different about the girl this morning, although the fishwife couldn't put her finger on it. As she told her sister later, 'it's as if the girl's soul had departed, and all that was left was her body'. Her sister nodded. She understood exactly what Mrs Landon meant.

"My ma has thrown me out of the house," whispered Freya.

"And why now, lass? What happened?"

Freya shrugged her shoulders and looked down at her feet. Mrs Landon knew that she wouldn't get any explanation out of her.

"I have nowhere to go," muttered Freya.

"I am sure that you will patch things up with your ma. All families argue."

Freya shook her head.

"She said that she hates me, wishes I'd never been born and I'm never to see her ever again."

Looking so traumatised, Mrs Landon knew that Freya had not made it up.

"Well, get your apron on. We will work it out by tonight, you'll see," the fishwife cajoled as she heaved the next barrel of fish over to the gutting table, and a faint smile flickered on Freya's face.

It was an awful day. It was raining, and the water ran down the hill towards the harbour. Once there, it would create a soup of fins, scales, and blood, which would stink to high heaven by morning. With an aching back, stood in silence battered by the bitterly cold weather, a desperate Freya longed to sleep, although she knew not where. Her mind raced as she reached for the last few fish. What would happen to her tonight? Her brothers would find her a lot more easily if she was forced to sleep out. It was then Mrs Landon finally spoke.

"You can stay with me."

A grateful Freya followed Mrs Landon out of the harbour and through the narrow back alleys of Polperro. It was the first time that she noticed how stooped and aged the old woman was. Her black skirt dragged along the cobbles, and the hem was frayed to tatters. Her hands had seen decades of hard work, and they were calloused and wrinkled, like those of an old sea dog. Mrs Landon always covered her head. Except for a few grey strands of hair here and there, Freya had no idea what the woman looked like without a bonnet. Every garment that she wore was black, and it remained so, winter and summer, Sunday to Sunday.

The old fishwife stopped at a tiny door and inserted the key into the black lock. She smiled at Freya and showed her in. The woman lived in a tiny room the size of a mouse hole with hardly any space to move. It was both small and crowded. Freya looked around her, and the word 'nest' came to mind. In an instant, the girl felt both warm and safe. A bed was pushed into a corner and covered with knitted blankets in bright colours. There were multiple carpets on the floor, and the furniture was pretty.

"My ma was rich," said Mrs Landon. "All this stuff belonged to her."

Freya nodded silently and continued to stare.

"What happened to her?" Freya asked.

"Come now, lass, we will not talk about the old days. There's no need to look up a dead horse's backside to see why it died, is there? What's done is done. I think we should treat ourselves to something nice for dinner. It is New Year, after all, yes?"

Together, they ate a simple but tasty dinner of bread and cheese.

"You take the bed tonight, Freya," Mrs Landon offered as they slurped on a cup of sugary tea that acted as dessert.

Although grateful, one of Freya's last thoughts before she fell asleep in the strange bed was that the market would be a stinking mess in the morning. This knowledge brought her to the realisation that her childhood was over. The days of stories and lullabies at bedtime were gone forever. She no longer had a ma or pa to care for her. She was alone and had to fend for herself. Freya was terrified.

Mrs Landon had no qualms about Freya staying with her indefinitely. The girl gave her no trouble at all. She worked hard and was very quiet at home. Mrs Landon wasn't sure if quiet was the correct word to describe Freya. She preferred to use the word 'vacant'. Freya displayed no signs of curiosity or creativity. She would never be found chatting and laughing with the other girls who worked at the fish market, and she had no social life. She seldom showed emotion or enthusiasm. All these strange characteristics were gathered into a bouquet of negativity, and once again, Freya was labelled 'odd'.

*

Freya's brothers were humiliated. She had shown them up in front of the men on the boat, and they had lost most of their loyal crew, only the rogues remained. The Wagners had ordered the fishermen to throw Samson's body overboard, hoping that the corpse would sink without trace, but the men were nervous that Samson Derry's bloated and buoyant body would wash up on the rocks.

One man in particular put the frighteners on his fellow deckhands.

> "And that means that the coppers will get involved. There will be questions, and eventually, the truth will come out."

It's often difficult enough for two people to keep a secret. For the brothers, trying to shut up thirty-or-so men would be impossible. Samson had boasted in the pub that he was doing some work for the Wagner boys and that he intended on investing his share of the spoils in a whore and a bottle when he next returned.

Samson was a brute of a man with a violent past, and his dastardly reputation followed him wherever he went. The Wagner brothers were delighted to employ a man of his calibre and he proved to be their greatest asset. Samson's cruelty knew no bounds, and he drove fear into the heart of any man who crossed the Wagners. He usually targeted the errant man's wife and children, going as far as to molest them when a little more persuasion was necessary. The Wagners knew that his disappearance would eradicate the sinister power they held in St Ives and that a lot of men would take the opportunity to avenge themselves and their families. The brother's stranglehold over the community was gone.

It was Klaus's pride that ultimately got the better of him. The more he thought about Freya, the more he seethed. With his brothers' permission and blessings, Klaus set out for Polperro. He planned to follow his sister home from work and ambush her.

"I'll drag her into an alley and slit her throat," he conspired with them.

Klaus was adamant about doing a good job of it too. The little git wouldn't escape what was coming to her this time.

"At four o'clock on a wintery afternoon, it will be nice and dark. It's going to be easy to hide somewhere and wait," he explained.

"Providing you can keep your big ugly mug out of the market and the drinking holes," warned a patronising Stefan.

When Klaus reached Polperro, he soon found a little nook where he could look over the harbour. In cold weather, the fish market occupied a warehouse on the wharf. After the sunset, Klaus's discomfort grew. Tiring of waiting, he became irritated, which then became fury. It was miserably cold, and it was raining. The nook turned into a waterlogged hell-hole and Klaus was soon ankle-deep in a murky puddle. He looked up to the grey sky. Big fat raindrops stung his face. There was no sign of the rain abating.

He removed a small hip flask from his coat pocket and drank the contents with gusto. The alcohol didn't improve his mood, but it did give him reckless bravado as he whispered to himself to keep up morale.

"Yes, I'll go into the warehouse. Pull my collar up and my hat down. I'll blend in and stalk her that way. Easy"

The instant that he lay eyes upon Freya, Klaus lost all sense of self-control. Business was slow because of stormy weather, so Mrs Landon had gone home to put on a casserole, leaving Freya to work the stall alone. A sinister grin shaped Klaus's lips as he lowered his hat brim and walked over.

Freya was busy scraping some stray scales off a fish when she sensed a person behind her and turned around to help the customer. It didn't matter that Klaus had attempted to disguise himself because Freya recognised the fiend immediately. Her normally vacant eyes widened, and a myriad of thoughts went screaming through her head, then she calmed down, knowing that she wouldn't survive the day if she was hysterical. Still holding the large knife, she remembered how she'd felt when she defended herself from that ogre, Samson, who planned to rape and murder her just a few weeks back.

Freya spoke first, which surprised Klaus.

"What do you want here?"

Freya spoke quietly, not wanting to draw attention to herself. People had started to pack up for the day, and the market was almost empty.

"Your doings have almost crippled our business," said Klaus.

"It was your own doing."

"Don't be short with me, you ugly little cow. You will not live to see the new day."

"Don't threaten me, Klaus. Get out."

Klaus reached out and grabbed his sister by the sinewy forearm. He put one hand on the oak barrel to steady himself and pulled her towards him with the other. The warehouse's higgledy-piggledy flagstones had made the bully more vulnerable than he realised. He squeezed Freya's thin limb, with every intention to break it. She felt the pain travel up her arm, the nerves carried the agony through the muscles of her neck. Finally, it reached her brain, where it exploded into savage fury. Faster than the eye could see, she raised the arm that was holding the knife and brought it down with superhuman force. She plunged it into the top of Klaus's hand resting on the barrel. She felt some resistance as it went through the bones, but the rest of the blade's journey was effortless, until it stopped dead when the handle rested against his rough skin. With his hand pinned to the barrel, he couldn't move. Klaus knew that if he cried out, he would draw attention from the last-minute stragglers at the market. It wasn't a mortal wound, but there was a lot of blood, and it began to seep into the wood of the barrel.

"Don't call out," she whispered in Klaus's ear.

Klaus was too shocked to respond.

"Klaus, I am warning you, be alert because you will lose your life," she told him. " I am going to kill you one day. You mark my words, dearest brother. Watch your every step because I will come for you when you least expect it. Keep watching over your shoulder, listen for footsteps behind you, because one day I will get the opportunity to slaughter you like a pig. Then I will stand back and gleefully watch you die. And when I am finished with you? I will do the same to Karl and Stefan. Consider me the angel of death."

Freya saw the terror in her sibling's eyes, and it empowered her. Looking pale, he tried to pull the knife out of his hand, but she held it firmly and wiggled it about to increase his suffering and emphasise her contempt. Klaus had never been on the receiving end of torture, and he wanted to faint. She waggled it again. Blackness smothered Klaus. He slid to the floor, one hand pinned to the wood as if he was crucified.

When Klaus regained consciousness, he was lying in fish entrails, and his hand was ripped to shreds. Freya was gone, and her cruel streak was finally liberated. It had thrilled her to see the terror in her wicked brother's eyes. Even though he didn't beg for mercy, she delighted in watching him writhe, and she fed off his agony. Not only was she spiritually dead, but she was also becoming a remorseless monster like her brothers. She felt satisfied with what she'd become, no longer weak, meek and pushed around. She felt relieved, enlightened, and she embraced the knowledge that her ugly black soul now matched her ugly face.

*

Freya went directly to Mrs Landon's house. She wasn't scared to walk on her own for once. She didn't scour the shadows, and she didn't run. Mrs Landon looked up as Freya stepped into the small room.

"You're late, lass," the old woman greeted with a cheery smile. "You have to be starving after such a long day. Let me get you a bowl of my nice casserole. That'll put you right."

The steaming bowl of nourishment arrived, but Freya pushed it aside. Mrs Landon ignored the gesture and continued to natter on, but the girl had no desire to participate in small talk. Instead, she decided she would be direct and tell Mrs Landon exactly what had happened. The old woman had been good to her, and as ruthless as Freya had become, she had to tell the truth. It was the right thing to do.

"I have to leave immediately, Mrs Landon."

The old fishwife frowned, wondering if she'd heard correctly.

"Leave? Why would you want to leave? Are you unhappy here? Have I done something wrong? Are you getting married?"

"No. My brother Klaus Wagner arrived at the market this evening. He threatened to kill me.

Finish the job he began in the harbour. So, I stabbed him."

"Stabbed? Is he dead?" Mrs Landon gasped.

Freya gave her an abridged version of the story.

"No, he's alive. That means he and the others will come for me, sure as the sun rises in the east."

"Well. I am stunned. How can I help you, lass? Tell me. Anything. Just ask."

"I cannot involve you in this matter. They will hurt you if they know I am living here. You are at risk with me in your house."

"Where will you go?" Mrs Landon asked her.

"I don't know, but I am not afraid. I will find my way."

Mrs Landon noticed that there was a distinct change in Freya. She was still distant but displayed a confidence that the woman had never seen before.

"I'll find a village east of Callington."

"There's hardly anything out there, lass. You won't find work out there, especially with your family reputation."

"Then perhaps Devon?" Freya replied.

"No, you need to be far away from a town if you're going to keep your head down."

The old woman paused and became thoughtful.

"I am going to send you to my sister. She lives on Bodmin Moor. Her cottage is a good distance from Bodmin, the town. Very remote. I'll give you a letter and ask her to take you in. You will leave before sunrise and take the old path north, not the new road. I will write down directions to my sister's farm."

"Thank you," Freya said, wondering if she would accept the offer.

"You'll be safe there. She leads a different life to me. You'll see what I mean when you meet her, but don't be afraid. She is a kind person in her own odd way."

Freya packed her bag. There wasn't very much inside it. She put in a few items of clothing, and Mrs Landon insisted that she take a blanket to keep warm. When the woman turned her back, Freya put her hand in her pocket and pulled out the small bloodied penknife and oil stone. As she wiped the blade clean on a rag, she was calm. When the soft comforting glint of the metal re-emerged, she told herself she wasn't lonely anymore. She would never be lonely again. The knife was her best friend.

Mrs Landon kindly packed enough food to last her two days. She wrapped it in newspaper.

"Here. It will be a long walk to Bodmin Moor. I want you to be safe."

The thought of the journey ahead had numbed Freya's appetite, but she accepted it anyway.

> "Avoid people. Don't speak to anyone on the road, lass. Promise me you won't tell anyone your story. No one needs to know who you are."

Freya left an hour before sunrise, which meant Polperro would be far behind her by dawn.

> "Now be on your way, lass."

> "Thank you for everything that you have done for me," said Freya with a rare surge of sincerity.

> "Not at all, lass, not at all. Be off with ye now, and don't look back."

As she trudged off, Freya identified the irony in her thoughts. 'Look back? Who cares? It makes no difference. I understand my lot in life—and I'm already as caustic and lifeless as a pillar of salt.'

5

THE CUNNING WOMAN

"My name is Selene," the woman introduced herself, "you can call me Lene."

"Freya," said the girl, extending a hand.

Selene studied the visitor and her accompanying note for a while.

"I like the name, Freya. It will take you far in my world."

Freya frowned, confused.

"Love and death, an interesting combination," Selene mused, then smiled wryly.

"What do you mean?"

"You have been named after a Norse goddess, my dear, the goddess of love, fertility, battle, and death."

Mrs Landon was correct. She and her sister were indeed different. The fishwife was humble and modest, whereas Lene was bold and flamboyant, and a sense of mystery enveloped her. Lene's long grey hair wasn't scraped back into a bonnet, it hung around her weathered face. The grey tresses were wild and untamed, yet she didn't look like a hag. Freya would have described her as someone of the earth. She had bright eyes and a broad smile, and her teeth were perfect, which in itself was unusual for a woman of that age. She had a ring on every bent, wrinkled finger. Most of them were copper, with strange engravings, but on the forefinger of her right hand was a gold ring with a large ruby. It was an ostentatious piece, and you couldn't help but notice it. She observed Freya ogling the ring.

"It was my mother's," she offered. "My father served in India. He brought it back as a gift for her. I inherited it because I was the eldest daughter. Believe me when I tell you that my sisters never forgave me for accepting it. They would have preferred that I sell it and share the money. It is very valuable."

"How many sisters do you have?" Freya asked.

"Five, including Elsa," Lene said, referring to Mrs Landon. "She's the only one who still talks to me. The rest followed their husbands and left here when they married."

Freya studied Lene's clothing. Her skirt reached her ankles. It had been patched and re-patched with bright pieces of cloth. To Freya, it resembled a tattered rainbow with a lot of character. Lene's shoes were flat leather lace-ups, and although it was cold, she wore no socks.

For all Freya's newfound boldness, she was caught off guard, she'd never met a woman as unconventional as Lene before, and she found herself on the back foot.

Lene's farm was nothing more than a muddy plot, with a tumbledown barn. At least the accompanying thatched-roofed cottage was reasonably decent. A few chickens were scrubbing in the dirt. Two rambunctious dogs tearing about the yard made a beeline for the newcomer, jumping up at her, threads of saliva stretching from their jowls as their gaping mouths barked.

"The dogs are Romulus and Remus," laughed
Lene. "They are fiercer than they look."

Freya took in every detail around her and smiled. The isolated location seemed perfect for her to plan retribution undetected.

"I'm glad to see you like it here. Now, why are we standing out here talking?" Lene chortled with a cheery laugh sounding much younger than her advancing years. "Let's go and natter over a cuppa."

*

Lene opened the door to the crooked cottage. The words of the old nursery rhyme came back to Freya:

"There was a crooked man
Who walked a crooked mile..."

It looked as if the thatched roof was well taken care of because there were no holes to be seen. A chimney gently puffed out smoke, promising that the inside of the remote dwelling would be homely.

The cottage was as cosy as Freya had anticipated. Lamps were hanging here and there against the stone walls, and the golden light bounced off the copper pots that stood on a rickety dresser, giving the room a warm glow. Against the wall stood a large, black, iron stove, which emitted the delightful heat. Colourful crocheted blankets were draped over pretty, but worn chairs. Freya guessed that they, too, were part of the family inheritance, much like Mrs Landon's furniture. Although the room was a significant size, to one side was a deep red velvet curtain pulled shut, dividing the room in half.

Although structurally sound, the interior of the rest of the cottage was in a state to behold. Freya had never seen a house so untidy. The small kitchen table was littered with bottles and jars and surrounded by what looked like weeds.

"You can sleep there," said Lene, pointing at a narrow cot pushed up against the wall.

"I have a down quilt that will keep you warm at night. Use the cushions that are lying about. It really doesn't matter which ones you choose. Make yourself comfortable."

The stove was a mass of bubbling saucepans. Jars of strange wizened herbs and gnarly brown bark littered every surface. Freya's curiosity got the better of her, and she plucked up the courage to ask Lene what she was cooking. A loud laugh resonated throughout the room.

"Oh, lass, I think my sister didn't explain my profession."

"Which is?"

"You see, people refer to me as a 'wise woman—'"

Freya was taken aback. She had an inkling what a 'wise woman' was because her mother had always warned her to stay away from them and that they were 'almost as evil as the gypsies'. They were also referred to as 'the cunning folk.' Her mother's opinion was that 'they were nothing better than witches who cast spells.'

"—and your mother likely warned you against people like me." Lene stated rather than questioned.

Freya was at a loss for words. How could this woman she met minutes ago possibly have known what she was thinking?

"I would have been burned at the stake a hundred years ago," she chuckled as she prodded at the contents of a saucepan. "It's a good job all that business is finished with, I can tell you."

Freya's eyes moved to the scarlet curtain.

"Oh, that!" said Lene. "That's where I do a lot of my work. Go on, take a look. There are no secrets in this house."

She went to the drape and touched it hesitantly then sensed the rich pile of the velvet on the back of her hand. The fabric felt as luxurious as it looked. Freya drew the curtain aside swiftly as if she was expecting to find an intruder. She was disappointed. There was nobody there. Instead, as her eyes adjusted to the gloom, she found herself looking at a round, ornately carved, gothic-like, table with six matching ebony chairs. Although posh and imposing, it was also beautiful.

There were no windows in the little annexe, and the walls were black. There was a poor, rustic shelf nailed to a wall, and it was crowded with used tallow candles. Freya's trepidation was replaced with fascination. The space was small and intimate, yet definitely mysterious.

"There's nothing to be afraid of," Lene whispered in reassurance. "Sometimes the living need advice that they cannot get in this world."

"You call up—"

Freya couldn't say the word.

"Spirits?" Lene said, completing the sentence for her.

Without being aware, Lene studied Freya's face and saw no signs of fear. The wise woman pointed to the weeds on the table.

"Plants and herbs. The earth gives us everything to heal ourselves."

She watched as Freya's eyes travelled to the little jars.

"Ah, yes," was all Lene said and didn't proceed to tell her guest anything more about them.

Freya sensed that Lene wanted to change the subject, which prickled her curiosity even more.

Lene pushed some pans to one side and set the kettle on the stove for tea. She took the bread out of the cupboard and a large salted ham wrapped in crispy parchment paper. Both the bread and the ham were hewn into large chunks with Lene's biggest knife. Ravenous, Freya wolfed down the ham. Then she took the large lumps of bread, dipped them in the tea, and ate it.

"Would you like more?" asked Lene.

Freya nodded.

> "The poorer people pay me in food, you see. I have a permanent stock of fruit and vegetables. There is a cow in the barn, and we get eggs from those scruffy hens you saw prancing about. Robert Cousins delivers flour and salted meat from my well-to-do callers. You'll not be hungry under this roof. If you want to spend a penny, there is a long drop lav out the back, and a big basin in the barn where you can wash."

Freya cleaned the dishes and dried them on a grubby looking cloth.

> "Good," Lene told her. "That will be your job from now on. I have no visitors tonight, so why not have a wash and climb into bed. We have a lot to do tomorrow."

*

As the days progressed, Freya became more and more interested in Lene's craft, especially since they had a lot of visitors. She would take them behind the rich red curtain and give Freya instructions to stay on her cot and never interrupt her.

There was a vast array of different people that came and went. Some were humble folk who arrived and paid Lene with comestibles that they could ill afford to give away. Others were sophisticated visitors who spoke the Queen's English who tended to arrive late at night to hide their occultist habit under the cover of darkness.

When those aristocratic clients arrived, Lene would hasten them into the cottage, whisper furtively, and usher them into the dimly lit room, then scurry behind the curtain with her charge. Everything would begin in whispers, but sometimes raising the dead could become quite a noisy business.

For the first month or two, Freya obeyed Lene, but inevitably her curiosity got the better of her, and she began to sit next to the curtain and strain her ears to hear what was happening behind the enigmatic red screen.

*

One rainy afternoon while Freya was washing the dishes and Lene was brewing foul-smelling potions, she suddenly addressed the girl.

"Would you like to become an apprentice of the darker arts, Freya?"

Without any hesitation, she accepted the position, presuming the apprenticeship would prove to be far more powerful than the knife.

Freya studied with Lene, learning how to make every potion and talisman. She committed to memory how to heal and create charms for both good and evil. Tarot cards and reading the future fascinated her, but the greatest thrill was calling up spirits and laying them to rest.

It didn't take long before Freya identified Lene's subtle yet authoritative manner. She coaxed people to trust her, and she drew more information from them than they realised. Her readings were cryptic, often confusing, yet the seeker always gleaned satisfaction from her revelations. But Lene was also crafty. She would spend a good deal of time drawing local gossip from her visitors, then she would use the newfound knowledge to predict future events.

Freya had to concede that Lene did have the gifts of a medium because she'd witnessed her resurrect disturbing apparitions. People were both desperate and fearful of speaking to souls that had exited the earthly dimension. Lene would first settle her patrons' tortured souls by preparing them for what would happen during a séance. She would calmly tell them that there is nothing to fear, and that the souls could not harm them. After this, she would continue to lead them through the taboo practice of spiritualism. She would talk of only the body of a person dying, and that the spirit is pure energy that longs to live on. Lene would eradicate all their fears and hesitations of raising the spirits of lost children, parents and husbands, by assuring that she only welcomes friendly communications.

This trust, accompanied by deep affection, emboldened Lene's clients to return again and again.

In one session, Lena called out for the spirit to make its presence known. Her chair creaked, but then there was a strange thud and some curious rumbling followed. The visitor gasped at the proof their loved one had made contact.

It was then Freya spotted an apple roll out from under the drape, secretly clasped between Lene's knees earlier to be deployed when needed for maximum effect.

Freya never discussed her observations with Lene. She simply sat back and watched the woman over the coming weeks.

Lene taught Freya about herbal medicine, which was mildly successful in healing the sick. Lene disclosed the contents of the tiny jars, which were far more sinister than everything the girl had learned to date. They contained human and animal tissue: fingernails, hair, fur, bones and the like. Horrible smelling liquids made from the decayed hearts and livers of animals. The more the potions stank, the more the visitors believed in the power of their dark magic.

Lene had ancient books with recipes containing the horrific ingredients, and Freya read it from cover to cover, again and again. Soon, she was adept enough to be introduced to Lene's patrons.

"I am mentoring Freya to follow in my footsteps."

The ever-creative Lene designed an enchanting backstory for the new recruit, which would further entice the desperate to seek her skills. She told them that Freya had arrived at her farm, in a wired and dishevelled state, clinging on to life. She had been on the run from attackers, who, when Freya had so desperately wished death upon them, came into a fatal accident by way of a drunken fall into a worker's hole. Freya had continued to run, cold and starving, to Lene's house. Lene said that she felt Freya had been kept alive only by some mysterious power that must have meant she was destined for the arts. This story had the visitors captivated.

*

Robert Cousins delivered the letter on a dismal Friday afternoon. Lene's eyes filled with tears when she read it.

"Elsa's gone," she told Freya. "She died peacefully in her sleep last night. I didn't have time to say goodbye to her."

"I am sorry," said Freya, feigning compassion. "Perhaps if you try and contact her, you can?"

Lene wiped away her tears and looked into Freya's eyes.

"You know it is all a sham, Freya. You are astute. I am sure you have identified it as such."

Freya nodded.

"There is no way across the chasm between life and death. It is too dark, deep and wide. I don't know if I will ever find her."

'That statement was true,' was Lene's underlying thought. Still, occultism seemed a lucrative business to her, so Freya had no qualms about exploiting desperate people.

6

THE INHERITANCE

The wise woman was impressed with Freya's rigorous dedication to her craft and the extra help was welcome. Lene had felt increasingly lethargic since the news of Elsa reached her. She couldn't identify the cause of the malaise and was forced to accept that she needed some rest if she was to regain her gumption. The sorrow she felt at her sister's passing was exacerbated by the constant fatigue. Relieved that Freya was there, Lene soon had the girl doing everything. Grateful, she paid Freya well, and soon her gifted minion accumulated a healthy little nest egg.

Winter was turning into spring. Heavy fog drifted over the moor, camouflaging the land with a wet, white shroud. It was almost midnight, yet nobody had come to the cottage that evening. Lene and Freya sat in the warm glow of the lamps, their hands cupped around their tea.

"I have no children," Lene told Freya. "Didn't want any either. Never met a man I wanted to be with, I suppose."

The girl said nothing and left Lene to talk.

"Freya, I want you to know that if I die, I am leaving this cottage and the plot, with all its bits and pieces to you."

"But, why?" asked a genuinely astonished Freya.

"Like I said, I have no children. You deserve all this. You could have exposed me a long time ago, but you haven't. I am grateful to you for being loyal."

Freya couldn't believe what she was hearing. She'd never anticipated this, and it came as a great surprise.

"Thank you, Lene," said Freya in a humble tone that belied her calculating mind. "It means a lot to me."

"Be a dear and open the curtain up, will you?" asked Lene, pointing to the wall of red.

Freya drew the drape aside.

"Now, get under the table. There is a loose floorboard. Pull it up," Lene giggled. "I have always hidden my money there," she boasted confidently. "Nobody will ever search under it— they are too afraid of ghosts."

Freya pushed and pulled. Soon, the plank loosened, and she twisted it out of the groove. Beneath was a sturdy steel box with a large padlock dangling from it . It was probably what Lene wanted to show her, so she lifted it from the hole. She gave Lene the box and watched the woman take a long chain out from under her skirt. Twinkling at the end of it was the shiny yellow key for the lock. There was an ever so gentle click as she released the lock and threw open the lid.

"There is a lot of money in here," she told Freya.

Now, the old woman had all of Freya's attention.

"This is the cash I inherited from my parents and most of the proceeds I made throughout my life here," she explained with a nostalgic smile.

Freya looked at Lene in wide-eyed wonder.

"I decided to save it rather than spend it all. Not missed out mind. I've still had a lot of fun.. Isn't that what life is all about, Freya? I can't be doing with hoity-toity townsfolk and their rules. I'd rather lead a happier, simpler life out here."

She put her hand on the girl's arm affectionately.

"There are a few thousand pounds in this box, Freya, and some jewellery. When the time comes, take it and do something good with it. Leave this god forsaken moor and its isolation, find a good man, have a family," Lene told her.

Freya nodded, but she couldn't pry her eyes away from the box.

"Now put it back, lass. You know where to find it if something happens to me."

Freya replaced the box where she'd found it and put the plank back where it belonged. Lene was tired and went to her bed. Freya climbed onto her cot, pulled the bedclothes over her, but couldn't fall asleep. Lene's words went around and around in her head: 'If something happens to me. If something happens to me. If something happens to me'.

Freya only fell asleep once she'd decided what she was going to do, and it didn't take a lot of thought. The time was ripe to hasten her plan, and she would begin the next day.

*

Dependable Robbie Cousins continued to deliver supplies twice a week, but every time he asked to see Lene, Freya told him that she was very ill and needed to rest. Freya was telling the truth. Lene was very sick—she was slowly being poisoned by her apprentice.

On Robbie's third visit, Freya allowed him to see the landlady and it stunned the lad to see that the feisty, cheerful woman he knew so well had deteriorated to such an extent that she could hardly talk. Freya knew that Robbie would return to Bodmin and tell everybody that Lene was on her last legs, which was precisely what she wanted. She wanted to create the expectation of Lene's imminent death so that there would be no surprises when Robbie returned to Bodmin with the news that Lene was no more.

*

Heavy spring rain set in. The moor had turned to marsh, and the roads were flooded. In such perfect conditions, it only took Freya four days to dig the six-foot hole where she would bury Lene. Halfway down, she hit the water table, but she couldn't risk burying Lene in a shallow grave. Freya dug through the sludge, rock and mud and spent hours emptying the water hole just to have it flood again. It was backbreaking work, but she was determined to have the body in the ground before the rain subsided.

Of late, Lene couldn't lift her head off the pillow. She knew that she was being poisoned, but she was too weak to do anything about it. Looking muddy and windswept, Freya came into the room and looked down at Lene, and their eyes met.

"Why?" croaked Lene.

Freya put her head back and began to snigger. It turned into a laugh and then the shrill cackling sound of a lunatic.

"Oh, Lene," she giggled, "don't you know the saying, my dear? 'One man's bread is another man's poison?'"

Still laughing, Freya's body shook with delight.

"You are evil," groaned Lene.

"People have always told me that."

The light in Lene's eyes began to fade and she uttered her last rasping words.

"Freya. The goddess of love and the goddess of death. Except that you have no love. You have hidden your cruel temperament from me for all these years, and I curse you for it."

"I was cursed long before you met me," whispered Freya. "You cannot take credit for where I go beyond this world."

With that, Freya yanked out Lene's pillow and thrust it on her face. The woman's body was so weak that she didn't have the strength to object.

Some of the locals knew Lene had willed everything to her loyal lodger, including the contentious ruby. When Freya was sure that the woman was dead, she removed all the rings from her fingers and put them on her own. She left the ruby till last and put it on the forefinger of her right hand. It looked wonderful.

*

Still in need, the locals continued to approach Freya for her services. Whereas Lene was warm and friendly, Freya was aloof and dark. Word had it that she had a gift for brewing potions and casting spells that made her predictions accurate, and soon, she developed a reputation as a powerful medium too.

The callous and calculating girl had taken to going into Bodmin once a week. She was a brilliant observer and while she stood in the markets pretending to need supplies, she would eavesdrop on conversations that may be of benefit to her. This precise information, names, places, traits, dates and the like, made manipulating her desperate clientele so much easier. Patrons fell for all the eye-opening details subtly weaved into her predictions, confirming they needed Freya's mystical guidance to improve their lives, whether in business, hate or love. Using this sly method for gathering intelligence, her business grew tenfold.

Gaining an underground reputation for being mistress of the dark arts, nobody visited Freya's cottage during the day. That would have caused consternation amongst the non-believing townspeople. Tortured living souls would slink over at the dead of night and sit behind the scarlet curtain, waiting upon Freya to divine their future. Somehow, hearing the predictions under the cloak of darkness made the readings and predictions even more believable.

*

It was impossible for Freya Wagner to hide her identity. Lene had always referred to her by her birth name, and she was revered, infamous and famous. So far, the Wagner brothers knew where she was, but they ignored her. The rumours of her developing the powers of a wise woman enabling her to harm them from a distance offered a further level of protection above her violent streak. Lene's network of believers stretched far and wide throughout Cornwall, then as far as Devon and on to the borders of Wales. Inevitably, the news of Lene's death reached the brothers' ears, and so did the rumour that she'd willed everything to Freya.

Not wanting to dirty or lose his hands, Klaus chose a man to watch Freya. He was slight, his demeanour was unthreatening, and he was a wizard with a knife.

> "I want to know how much she has, where she keeps it, and estimate how difficult it will be to get rid of her."

Bayswater Freddy nodded. London had become too small for him, and the villain had fled to Cornwall. It was the right place to be if the law came looking for him. There were plenty of mail ships travelling past the piece of jutting land. He could escape to any country in the world before dawn.

Klaus gave the city boy a gentle old nag, and watched him set off across the moors. It wasn't unusual for strangers to ask directions to Freya's abode, and when he reached Bodmin, the townspeople were happy to oblige. They looked the skinny man up and down, another 'down on his luck' or lovestruck soul, or perhaps, he had treated someone badly and was searching for redemption.

Freddy saw the cottage in the distance. The yard was quite neat, and the only sign that it was inhabited was the ever-present puff of smoke from the chimney. He climbed off the horse, opened the wooden gate and led it into the yard.

As if by magic, an apparition appeared behind Freddy. He jumped, taken aback. He had not seen the woman when he entered the yard.

"You here on business?" asked Freya.

"Erm, yes."

"Tie your horse over there at the gate, then come to the house."

Freddy did as he was told. With the horse tethered, Freya led him into the cottage by the arm. He saw the red curtain. It wasn't much different to his experience at a brothel. He smirked until Freya's icy stare told him his thoughts had been rumbled. Freddy looked around him at the bottles and potions, big bushels of herbs and garlic hung from the rafters. They distributed a pungent smell, and he felt that he couldn't breathe.

"Ten quid upfront," Freya said, thrusting out her hand.

"Why?"

"You might not like what I say when I'm done."

Freddy nodded and put a battered note on the table.

"What do you want to know?" Freya asked.

Freddy laughed.

"I want you to ask the spirits where you hide your money."

"Who sent you?" Freya asked coolly.

"Your brothers."

Freddy saw the big ruby ring amongst the others on her fingers and decided that he would pocket it when his job was done. Nobody would ever know about it.

She'd always planned for this eventuality, and Freddy didn't know what he was in for.

"Under the table," she answered.

Freddy frowned. He was confused. He had thought that she would put up more of a fight. Freya could see his face marked by confusion.

"The spirits told me that my brothers were sending you. That's why I was waiting for you at the gate."

Freddy felt the hair on the back of his neck rise.

"Don't try and trick me, you witch," said Freddy, unsure of himself.

Freya took the key from around her neck.

"Move the table. You will find it under the floor."

Freddy grabbed the key eagerly and pulled the table to one side. He dislodged the planks and found the box. He was in a hurry to open it, and when he did, he was so mesmerised by the wealth that it carried, he didn't notice Freya come up behind him.

Freya could have killed Freddy, but she needed him. The bloody club lay on the floor next to him, as he fought to breathe. It was clear that Klaus and the others had not learnt their lesson. She went to the kitchen and took out a chopping knife, and proceeded to cut hack at his fleshy fingers. Freddy felt the pain and started to come around. His hand was aching, and when he looked down, he realised that his thumb was gone.

Freddy screamed, pulled off his shirt, and used the tails to bind the wound. Freya moved towards him slowly. She had a little bottle in her hand, and she opened it. Inside was his thumb plus what looked like the claw of an animal, rotting and encrusted with blood. The smell was pure evil. She carefully added two tiny drops of inky black liquid into it, then sealed it and put it into the terrified Freddy's coat pocket, and gave it a couple of confident taps.

"Take this to my brothers. It is a curse. One of them will surely die."

Freddy was terrified. Although the pain was severe, the terror was worse, and he fled. Freya followed behind him. Her victim tore into the yard at the precise moment that Robbie Cousins arrived with the mail, and skipped off the cart, and gave a cheery 'hello'.

"Freddy is just on his way, Robbie. Would you care to give him a ride into Bodmin?"

"No problem with that, Freya," the lad replied.

"My horse." panted Freddy.

"That old nag is mine now. You were just dropping it off for me, weren't you?" snarled Freya as a pale-faced Freddy looked on agog. "Now, be gone with ye."

Freddy hid his bloodied hand deep in his coat pocket as he and Robbie trundled away from the cottage. The fingers on the ruffian's good hand felt the smooth cold glass vial resting in the darkness. Bayswater Freddy began to panic about what would happen if he passed the cursed container onto the Wagner brothers—and if he didn't.

*

Klaus Wagner looked at Freddy mockingly.

"Where's my horse, you lout?"

"She took it."

Klaus took a step forward, clamped his hand firmly on the quaking man's shoulder, then began to shake with laughter so much it was a struggle to speak.

"You—the notorious 'hard man'—Bayswater Freddy allowed a mere woman to get the better of you?"

Stefan and Karl joined in the merriment.

Freddy's hand emerged from his pocket and he unwound the dirty cotton bandage and held it up. Karl was the first to notice the missing thumb, cleanly severed at the joint.

"My working days are over now," lamented Freddy. "And that's not the only bad news."

The three brothers looked at each other, then observed Freddy taking the jar out of his other pocket. With reverence, he placed it on the table like a priest setting down a chalice.

"What's that?" asked Karl.

Freddy shrugged as Karl picked up the bottle and opened it, turned the bottle upside down, and shook it gently until the evil-smelling claw fell out. Worse, it was followed by the rotting flesh of Freddy's thumb. A little of the black liquid touched Karl's fingers, but he ignored it. It was then the smell hit them, and they all took several steps back. They looked at Freddy aghast. He only had one card to play.

"Your sister said she is cursing you. That stuff is a curse. One of you will die very soon."

"You'll be the one dying, Freddy," snapped Klaus

They were furious with him for bringing such a terrible omen to them. Despite the bravado they were deeply worried about the potency of Freya's power. With Samson dead, Klaus stabbed, and now this, who knew what would happen next. The brothers watched Karl struggle to wipe off the black drops. It stained his finger like ink. Attacking them with soap and water achieved nothing.

"Don't worry about it, Karl. It's just a bit of superstitious old tosh," Stefan reassured as he scrubbed his brother's finger almost raw.

The poison that Freya had brewed meticulously was slowly absorbed through his skin and into his bloodstream. Two days later, Karl became sick, his fever rose, and his bowels twisted. Writhing in agony, he died as the clock chimed midnight. Klaus and Stefan were beside themselves with fear. Each one secretly vowed that they would never touch their sister again.

The news travelled from village to village and soon Freya knew that one of her brothers was dead. She didn't care which one. The community was heartened to hear of Karl's death. Everyone was weary of their tyrannical rule, so much so that the daily newspaper refused to print an obituary, and the local vicar refused to perform a funeral service.

Back in her cottage, as night fell, Freya sat by the fire, gazing at the flames, smiling. The best thing she had learned from her industry was that people were afraid of death, and for as long as she could maintain the perception that she was capable of predicting it, she would be the most powerful person in Cornwall.

7

ARTHUR DICKSON

Arthur was a good man, but he was lonely. He had been born on the farm next to Lene's and was fond of his strange neighbour. He would often wander over to the fence to have a chat about this and that, eager to swap stories and have a chuckle.

His parents had passed away many years ago, and he found himself all alone, in the middle of Bodmin Moor with no one to talk to apart from his herd of cows. One afternoon while he was walking fences, he saw Freya pottering in her yard. He leaned against a fence post, waiting for her to see him. Freya would have gladly ignored him, but he waved his hand, flashed a beaming smile, and made it obvious that he wanted to greet her and have a few words.

"Good morning," he said brightly.

"Yes?" Freya snapped.

Artie was taken aback by her brusque reply.

"Sad about old Lene," he muttered, self-conscious.

"Yes."

"Managing here on your own then, are you?"

"Yes."

"Well, let me know if I can help in any way," Artie told her kindly.

"Yes."

Although they were neighbours, Artie felt he had somehow taken a risk speaking to Freya. He understood Lene's peculiar career choice, but the woman had always been kind and had a great sense of humour -but Freya, well, she seemed scary, intimidating even. It was as if she was already dead inside.

*

Although close to the coast, the snow lay thick on the ground during the unusually cold winter. Artie was out on the moor gathering his flock. He could see Freya's cottage in the distance, a small speck. Smoke was rising into the sky. As he gathered the ewes, he noticed that the plume was becoming darker. Then, he saw a flicker of orange close to the chimney and he was in no doubt that the thatch was on fire. He turned his horse and raced towards the little house.

Freya stood in the yard, looking up at the cottage. Dry kindling had shot embers up the chimney, and they had landed on the thatch. If it wasn't for the wet weather and snow, the roof would have been destroyed already.

"Get a ladder," Artie yelled at her as he galloped up to the gate.

Freya took her worn step ladder out and propped it against the outer wall. Artie sprang out of his saddle and raced up the rungs like a monkey up a tree.

"Pass me buckets of snow," he called down to her.

Freya filled a pail, clambered up and met him halfway. Artie emptied the contents onto the flames.

It took twenty minutes to extinguish the fire fully. Although it wasn't a blaze as such, it had caused sufficient damage that the roof would need serious mending.

"This would have been difficult if you hadn't been here," she said solemnly.

"You will freeze in that house tonight. You're welcome to sleep at my farm."

Freya didn't like the idea of anyone learning too much about her.

"No. I'll move to the barn. I'll be fine there. I'll take my old horse into town and find a thatcher in the morning."

"Tell you what," said Artie, "why don't I come over in the morning and patch things up. It won't be a perfect job, but it will do till spring."

Freya contemplated the offer. If Artie helped her, she realised she wouldn't need to mix with people in Bodmin, which finally gave one of his helpful suggestions some appeal.

"Agreed—"

She gave him an awkward half-smile and a nod.

"But, I will pay you."

"Of course, but we will talk about it later. I'd better get back to those sheep.

He turned to wave, but Freya was already gone.

*

Opening the door to the cottage, she looked about. The wind had whipped inside, and her tiny vials of treasured tinctures and potions were strewn across the place. The floor shone with a myriad of puddles where the melted snow had dripped through.

To Freya's surprise, Artie followed her into the small dwelling to see if there was any damage inside. He was greeted with devastation.

"You can't sleep here. It's late, and this place is chaos." Artie told her, ready to pack her and her bags into the cart and take them to his warm home.

"I told you I would be in the barn," dismissed Freya.

Artie had been kind to her, but she had no intention of becoming his friend. He shook his head at her. He had never met such a stubborn woman.

"Have it your way," Artie sighed. I will pop in in the morning and check up on you."

Freya had lied. She didn't sleep in the barn, she spent the entire night cleaning the cottage. She had no time to waste, having lost two days out of the working week already. She couldn't afford to lose any more business.

*

The next day, despite the stormy weather, Artie arrived at the cottage as promised, his trusty toolbox on the cart beside him. Although the wind was close to gale force, the helpful man planned to spend all the available daylight hours patching up the damaged thatch. He thought his kindness might thaw Freya enough for him to get to know her a little better. At the very least it would be nice to have a neighbour to chat to. He wondered if he had thought a little harsh of her yesterday. After all, she was dealing with a crisis, and unlikely to be a wonderful hostess.

Freya heard the crunch of the cart wheels, followed by him opening the gate. There was a short pause while he tethered his horse and then a knock on the front door. A hesitant Freya turned the handle then peered through the gap. She didn't really want a visitor and she didn't want to pay him. However, he had saved her cottage from a terrible blaze, so reluctantly she invited him in.

Artie looked around him, fascinated by all the bottles and bushels.

"Do you make medicine?"

"Sometimes," she replied.

"How do you know what to mix?" said Artie, inspecting the myriad of ingredients.

"Lene taught me."

"Yes, I miss our chats," Artie confessed. "She was a good soul."

Freya nodded but said nothing. As he shifted his weight from one foot to the other, it didn't look like Artie was about to tackle the roof any time soon.

"Tea?" she asked, hoping once he'd finished his cuppa he would make a start.

"Awe, that would be lovely," Artie said with a smile.

Freya made a brew and poured a cup for both of them.

"Lovely, thanks. This will warm my bones," he said, smacking his lips in anticipation.

She was surprised that Artie felt so at home with her. Nobody usually did. The large, jolly man showed a sincere interest in her, and she slowly began to relax in his company, wondering if he might be useful to her after all?

*

Artie would arrive at Freya's every Sunday afternoon at three o'clock on the dot. Alas, for Freya, the visits became a disruption not a delight, and she was increasingly annoyed that she'd accepted his help. Now, she owed him a debt of gratitude which he seemed keen to have repaid. She reminded herself repeatedly that if a similar situation occurred, she would hire someone from another town, a tradesman who was anonymous and far away. Freya didn't need to be a fortune teller to know that the relationship with Artie would end badly. The question was, when?

Artie's painful loneliness meant he had no such qualms and was wholeheartedly in love with the girl. As strange and distant as she was, his positive spirit immediately set about the task of healing her. In a surprise moment of tenderness and weakness, Artie took Freya in his arms and gently kissed her.

It was her first kiss and it had her flummoxed. She had engaged in every psychic and spiritual experience, but she never anticipated the lust that she would experience in the arms of a man. Keen to make a physical connection to cement their relationship, Artie tenderly encouraged Freya to undress them both.

Although the union was physically pleasant, Freya had broken the vow to herself. She'd allowed Artie to become far too familiar and attached to her, and develop feelings that would never be reciprocated. As soon as she had blown hot, Freya was now icy cold. She pulled away from him and barely said a word until he left. Then she decided enough was enough and to sever all ties with the poor fellow.

Artie couldn't understand what he had done. He so looked forward to seeing Freya on a Sunday afternoon, but now she refused to open the door to him. It took him four Sundays to realise that he wasn't welcome, and he was devastated. Freya would hear the knock on the door and ignore it. The first Sunday, the knocking sounded passionate. The second Sunday, it was desperate. Over two more Sundays, she heard it lose hope, and beyond that, she never heard it again.

*

In her mind, Freya Wagner never made mistakes, but two months later, she finally accepted that she was pregnant. This wasn't a problem, just a mistake. Soon a plan to rectify the error was afoot.

Freya asked Robbie Cousins to bring her a bag of barley the next time he came by, and he delivered it three days later. She broke off some of the kernels and put them in a warm damp place. Within three days, a thick mould had developed. She left it for another three, and on the sixth day, she ate the furry concoction. She'd given this to so many women who had come to her in desperation, and it had never failed to abort a foetus from the womb. This time it didn't, and Freya's discontent with her lot was raised another notch. Desperate, Freya took the dreadful mould for three days until she was at risk of poisoning herself to death. The parasite was determined to stay in her body, and Freya was furious.

*

Artie was dazzled when he opened the door and saw Freya. It was everything that he had hoped for.

"Oh, Freya, I knew you only needed time," he said, smiling joyfully.

Unfortunately, Freya's reply was as abrupt as ever.

"I am two months with child."

Artie gave a whoop and rushed forward to embrace her. Freya put out her hand and stopped him mid-stride.

"We will marry," Freya said mechanically.

"Of course, we will, my love. Me! A father at last!" gushed Artie, exuding joy.

"No. You misunderstand. I don't want my life disturbed by you. It's only to give the wretch a name."

Artie nodded his head, disappointed.

Two weeks later, early in the morning, they made their way into Bodmin. It was the first day of spring, and the countryside was living proof of the date. Pretty flowers popped up overnight, the sky was clear and crisp, and a watery sun had begun its fight towards summertime.

Freya sat next to Artie on the cart. Her face was unreadable. As was his nature, Artie was full of hope and chatted all the way to Bodmin in the futile hope that the mother of his child would warm to him if he showed sufficient cheer.

*

The parish clerk looked from Freya to Artie. He couldn't wait for them to leave so that he could tell everyone that the old witch had finally found a husband. Freya wrote her name at the bottom of the marriage certificate. It was the first time she'd signed any formal document, and Artie added his signature with an enthusiastic flourish. The clerk hurried them out of the office and flipped the sign on his door, 'closed from 12pm to 1pm'.

"Where will we celebrate?" Artie asked cheerfully.

"Nowhere. I want to go back to my cottage."

Artie grew very quiet. He was disenchanted. He had hoped that Freya would accept his kindness and recognise his dedication to caring for her and the child. That wasn't Freya's intention at all. Her sole intention was to try and remain less of a social pariah than she already was to drum up a few more client callers.

Freya returned to her home and Artie helped her off the cart and followed her to the front door.

"Go. I don't want you here. Is that clear enough for you?" Freya said, looking directly into his eyes.

Artie had no words. He just stared at Freya, until her cold eyes disappeared when she slammed the door in his face.

8

ISLA

Isla Dickson was born on the summer solstice. Freya delivered her baby alone. The child was one month premature and when she went into labour, Freya prayed that the child would die. It did not. Tempted to snap its vertebra and leave it for dead oft-times later, she wished she had. She took to leaving the child outside, unattended. Out of sight, out of mind, the practice afforded Freya some relief.

A week later, on his way past the cottage, Artie spotted his child nestled on an old sack bunched up in an apple crate. He picked up the tot and peered under the grubby, makeshift gown. A girl. She was the most beautiful baby he'd ever seen. Freya swooped out of the door like a silent dark ghoul.

"Has she got a name?" Artie asked, "she needs a name," he said, stroking his daughter's cherubic face.

"Yes. Gretchen. I am of German stock. You can register her when you go to Bodmin."

Artie scowled to himself and handed the small creature back to an ominous Freya. Instinctively, the babe turned her head to face her mother's bosom. Freya ignored the gesture.

"Is she feeding?" he asked.

"Yes," Freya replied, her voice bitter.

"I will come and visit her every d—."

"—No, you won't."

Artie looked at Freya, his happy demeanour fully dissolved. He grabbed the harpy by the arm and pushed her against the wall, his fire-red face close to hers.

"I will see my daughter every day, and don't think you will scare or sicken me with your mumbo jumbo."

Freya didn't reply, and Artie left the cottage yard, slamming the gate behind him.

*

Artie returned four days later. He had registered the child as Freya had instructed. He passed the document to his belligerent wife and took the baby from her.

"Hello, little Isla," he cooed, smiling.

Freya's head jerked up.

"What did you say?"

"Isla, her name is Isla. It was my mother's name."

Freya glared at him. She unfolded the birth certificate and felt her temper rise as her eyes skimmed across the small black word in the box. Artie was telling the truth. The baby had indeed been named Isla Mildred Dickson.

*

Little Isla had her father's happy disposition. She smiled all day, never cried and slept like a dream. Freya didn't even try to love the little girl. She was incapable. Freya only stopped short of hurting the child because the only pinprick of decency left in her dark mind reminded her what she'd suffered at the hands of her brothers. Plus, Artie visited every day to check up on the child and the visits were bound to be quicker if there was no concern for the child's welfare.

As Isla became older, Freya became more demanding and increasingly cruel towards the girl as she slowly began to practise painful discipline on her. The calculating and heartless mother was thoroughly unreasonable, giving Isla tasks that were impossible to complete and then beating her for not producing the 'expected' results.

Isla attended a school at the small parish church in the little hamlet of Treshop, which sheltered her from her mother's evil ways. Sadly, the girl had few friends because people were reluctant to befriend the 'witch's child'. In the end, things changed and the locals gave Isla, who was also Artie's daughter, the benefit of the doubt. Word had long since reached the community that Artie and his wife didn't live under the same roof, and they all agreed that Isla would be better off living with her doting father. Freya disagreed, enjoying the hurt she caused by separating Artie from his treasured offspring.

Through all of Isla's trials, she remained generous in spirit and kind in nature. She was her father's child. Nobody knew of the beatings that Isla endured at the bleak cottage on the moors, as Freya made certain that all the marks were under her daughter's dress—but nothing can be hidden forever.

*

As soon as Artie's horse recognised the road, he knew that he and his master were going to Freya's. The animal was never comfortable there, and would neigh and stomp nervously, showing clear signs of anxiety. Artie saw Isla from a distance and smiled. Oh, how he loved that child. He watched her walk from the field to the barn, struggling to carry a hoe, shovel and rake. It was late to be working, and the weather had turned cold. He noted Isla lacked a proper overcoat.

He opened the gate and led the spooked horse into the yard, its eyes becoming wild and terrified as it was tethered to the spot. He crept to the barn and opened the ramshackle door. It gave out a loud creak and a groan, its neglected steel hinges not oiled in a long time. Isla stood against a hay bale, wearing only her petticoat and bodice. She had her bare leg in a bowl of water and was rinsing mud off her shins. Her legs were a criss-cross of red stripes, and he wondered what she had done to herself. Each time she touched her skin she winced.

"What have you gone and done there? Did you get stuck in a fence?" Artie asked, trying to hide his concern.

"No, Pa," chuckled Isla, whose face lit up. "I fell in the mud and into a thorny bush. It's just a few scratches."

Artie turned away while she pulled her dress over her head and put on her boots. Once she was properly attired, she ran across the barn and hugged him.

"Show me them legs, then," said Artie.

Isla dodged the request.

"Honestly, it's nothing. Come now, Pa. Let's have a cuppa and catch up. Ma is passed out on her bed. There will be peace. I promise."

Artie ignored his daughter's ruse to distract him and gently pushed Isla, flopping her backwards onto a hay bale. He raised her skirt as far as her knee, then he inspected her. Both legs were a patchwork of old scars and new welts, clear evidence of thorns ripping through her flesh for quite some time.

"How long has this been going on?"

Artie's face was dark, the smile he was so well known for had left his face, and it was the first time that his daughter felt scared of him.

"Let it be, Pa. You know what she's like when she's mad."

"How long?"

"A long time, Pa, but it's alright."

"Go get a bag, lass. You are going to come and live with me."

"But Ma will be furious. She will make a lot of trouble for you— for us."

"I don't think so, my love. Go on, fetch your things."

Artie knew that he would be doing Freya a favour. She lacked any motherly instinct and never loved the child but was too proud and stubborn to send her away. It was obvious the miserable shrew hated the girl, but seeing her estranged husband living happily with his daughter was even harder to bear.

Without the steadying influence of the few people around her, Freya's decline towards lunacy became more palpable. Her only means of comfort was gin and she accepted that. It was pointless to put on a false front anyway. She knew that people were more afraid of death than they were of her. No matter what the gossips might say about her, she would always have a healthy clientele.

Keen to separate Isla from her mother's destructive influence, Artie decided to sell his farmstead and settle in a coastal town.

"Can we, Pa? Can we?" was Isla's delighted response.

The proceeds from the smallholding would keep him and Isla in good stead as long as they were frugal. A small house overlooking the harbour would bring peace to his soul, and he and Isla could begin a new life.

For Artie though, moving was not enough of a fresh start. He was determined to break off all his ties with Freya and approached the courts to assist him. Under duress, the magistrate made a trip to Freya Dickson's cottage. It was his duty to assess her mental capacity. Poor Artie had his fingers crossed. He could only divorce the merciless woman if she displayed lunacy.

*

It was a horrible day. The clouds hugged the land, and the wind was howling. The moors had a vast loneliness about them, and the magistrate would rather have been sitting in his comfortable chambers than bumping along a country road on his way to evaluate a mad woman. He had heard tales about the strange wise woman. While others consulted all kinds of people to foretell their future, he steered himself well clear of the valley of the shadow of death.

The magistrate's driver hopped off the cart, helped his master from the high wooden seat and escorted him to Freya's front door. His immaculate brown leather shoes squelched across the muddy farm yard, each step heightening his fury at the task in hand.

Freya opened the door. She was a spectacle. The legal man's educated mind was cast back to the opening lines of Macbeth.

"Yes?" she slurred, glassy-eyed, looking the magistrate up and down.

The man felt uneasy about the unearthly apparition in the doorway. He lost his tongue.

"You looking for help, sir? Yes? Come in."

Freya swung the door wide open.

The magistrate took a step into the cottage, his driver about to follow in his wake.

"Stay!"

Freya pointed at the floor like she was talking to a dog. The driver was livid. Even his snobbish master treated him with more respect.

The magistrate stood in the tiny space and his eyes watered from the foul smell of ammonia. Freya watched him pull up his nose.

"Distilled ox urine." she informed.

The smell stung the magistrate's throat as he fought back the instinct to vomit. He could imagine the foul stuff entering his lungs and diffusing into his blood. He looked at the red curtain, looking tattier than it did in Lene's day, and wondered what it was hiding.

"Do you want me to read your cards, sir?"

"No," snapped the magistrate, deciding that he would get to the point. He didn't have the stomach to be stuck in the stench and negotiate with a mad woman. He didn't need to enter into a lengthy dialogue to know that he agreed with Arthur Dickson. The woman was, without doubt, out of her mind.

"Your husband, Mr Arthur Dixon, wants to annul your marriage. Do you have any objections?"

"Nah," she drawled. "On what grounds?"

"He believes that you are mentally insane."

"Oh, he does, does he?"

The magistrate nodded.

"Are you going to put me in the madhouse?"

"Mrs Dickson, I am going to create the documents that will annul your marriage to Arthur Dickson. It doesn't take a doctor to diagnose you for the lunatic that you are, but I have no desire to drag you across Bodmin Moor kicking and screaming, and I am sure the tithe payers of the parish will thank me for keeping you out of an institution. If you remain out of trouble, I will ignore you."

Freya nodded, a mocking smile on her ugly face. She put her hand out to take the door handle. The magistrate saw the glistening red ruby on her forefinger.

"I recognise that," he said.

He noted a small flicker of annoyance in her eyes, but it was gone as fast as it appeared.

"It belonged to Lene. I knew her for many years. I liked her. An eclectic sort, but harmless enough, I suppose. How did you come by the ring?"

"She left it to me."

"She did? "

"Yes, in her will."

"Do you still have the document?"

Freya lied without batting an eyelid.

"It is here somewhere," she answered. "It's all legal and above board."

"Did you register her death?"

"It was bad weather, and then we had the winter. I did ask Robbie Cousins I think? Possibly? It was more than twelve years ago. What would it matter now?"

The magistrate nodded and smiled.

"Good day, Mrs Dickson. I will send my clerk to you with the relevant documents."

Freya didn't bid him farewell, preferring an icy stare to end the conversation.

"Make sure you close the gate properly," she shouted after the pair as they squelched away.

As the magistrate returned to Bodmin, the story of Lene's will troubled him. The only thing that seemed accurate in

Freya's account was that Lene had been dead for many years. It had been a slow and miserable journey back and when he reached his office at six, his secretary was waiting for him with a pile of papers to work through before he went home. Judging by the height of the stack, he wouldn't leave his office until eleven. As he waded through the first wave of dry details, he didn't give Freya Dickson another thought, and soon he pushed all his concerns about Lene's demise to the back of his mind too.

*

9

CHANGE OF FORTUNE

Although Artie lived frugally, he struggled to find work. He had only ever known farming, and life in the port of St Ives was vastly different to what he had envisaged. He and Isla had survived on the proceeds from the sale of the farm so far, but he knew that if he didn't invest in something, he would be broke within two years.

Their home was a small, two-roomed house in St Ives. Artie always laughed and told people that it was only fit for dwarves. Despite the cramped conditions, he and Isla were happy and they did the best they could with the little space they had. After living in the shadow of her miserable mother all her childhood, Isla embraced every day of freedom that God gave her with joy.

As young as she was, she managed to make the tiny rooms homely with some bright patchwork blankets and cushions. She and Artie kept their home spotless, and in the summer, the doors and windows were left wide open to capture the fresh smell of the sea.

It took some time for the townspeople to accept them - there had been 'talk'. Firstly, Isla's mother was a Wagner, and the Wagner family had a reputation for being wrong 'uns at best, ruthless villains at worst. Secondly, Isla's mother was said to be a witch, and people were so terrified of her that they warned their children never to look at her if she ever came to St Ives. Thirdly, everyone was suspicious of Artie - anyone who married a woman like that surely had a screw loose.

Over time the villagers realised that Artie was just a normal chap trying to give his daughter the best he could and that Isla was an adorable joyous free-spirited girl who always had a smile for anyone that passed. Artie was blessed that he could afford to send Isla to school, and she had discussed becoming a schoolteacher. Artie was so proud; his daughter was the joy of his life.

*

As with most bad ideas, Artie's demise began in the pub. Artie was a light drinker, so it wasn't alcohol that would complicate his life. It was his new friend Pete Fielding.

"What choice do you have, mate?" asked Pete. "You are stuck between a rock and a hard place, my friend. You have to make your savings work for you. 'Speculate to accumulate', they say, don't they?"

I'm a farmer, Pete. What do I know about running a shop?" replied Artie.

"I've been doing this for years. This little shop is a gold mine," Pete went on to explain.

Artie leaned in and listened carefully.

"It's easy, me old mucker. Buy cheap and sell high. No more to it. I wouldn't part with it, but the wife is determined to move up the coast to her sister in Wales. What the hell she wants to do in that tip is beyond me, but she has the thumbscrews on me mate. I have no choice. You know how it is."

Pete didn't explain that his wife was sick and tired of his shenanigans with other women, and she had served him with an ultimatum: he either changed his ways, or she would sell all their possessions and leave to live with her sister in Scotland. Although Pete liked carousing with women - all women - he loved his wife and couldn't live without her. Besides that, he was growing old, and these days it was hard work finding fresh prey.

"I am a prosperous man," Pete told Artie. "The hardware store has an excellent reputation. A little gold mine, I might say, if I should be so bold."

As Artie listened to the man, his enthusiasm got the better of him. He loved the idea and soon parted with all his savings, positive that he would recover his investment within two years.

Isla was beside herself with joy. She and her father would certainly make a roaring success of it.

"You know what, Isla. I am bursting with ideas on how to improve the hardware store. A lick of paint. Give the windows a buff and put things nicely on display. Pete says it already draws in all the locals who are tired of hoofing it over to Devon for what they need."

Within two hours of opening his new business, Artie heard the tinkle of the doorbell, and two men in black suits planted themselves firmly at the counter.

"We are from the debtor's court," the one said, without introducing himself.

"You have a debt to the value of £200," said the other.

Artie looked at them bewildered.

"You have a choice, Mr Dickson. You either pay your dues by the end of the month or be summoned to the debtor's court and spend a good few years as the guest of her majesty."

They threw a document across the counter.

"Sign it."

His hands trembled as his eyes scanned the text. He had been taken in, hook, line and sinker. His throat tightened as he panicked about his future. There was nothing for it though, it had to be signed. He felt his heart sink into his boots. He had not felt this dismal even when Freya rejected him.

Hamstrung, Artie approached the bank for a loan.

"We suggest you sell your home," the bank manager told him.

"But it is all that we own!" Artie exclaimed. "I would rather sell the business. Surely the stock and premises are worth something?"

"I am sorry, Mr Dickson. The business has not turned a profit in five years, which is why you are being sued for the debt."

"Can't they follow that scoundrel Fielding to Wales?"

"I can tell you without a doubt that Pete is long gone, he and his wife knew what was awaiting them, and they boarded a mail ship in Cardiff. They are well on their way to another country."

Artie stared at the man, speechless. He could hardly breathe. He couldn't even lose his temper. He was shocked.

"Unfortunately, when you purchased the hardware store, you also purchased the debt. That is the way of the law. It is taken for granted that the prospective owner studies the accounts carefully."

"Of course, you did Artie, you are a trusting man," the banker said kindly.

"What must I do," asked Artie. The situation was surreal. The truth had not yet sunken in.

"I can only suggest that you sell your cottage, and it is in a good position. There is no value in the hardware store. Nobody will invest in it."

Artie had always been a positive soul, but this day he went to his cheerful little home, sat on a chair, put his head in his hands and cried. He didn't cry for himself. He cried for his daughter. It was likely to change her future, and he was ashamed that it was due to the terrible mistake he had made.

*

"Oh, Dad," exclaimed Isla, "how terrible for you!"
She put her arms around Artie to comfort him.

Artie was overwhelmed by his daughter's grace and lack of judgement. She didn't ask him what he was going to do to rectify the situation, and she was only concerned about his well-being.

"Come now," she smiled, "no more of this nonsense, we will find a solution to the problem. I will find a job, and we will make do until you find work. You are not too old to begin an apprenticeship. Ask Mr Todd if he can teach you to fix nets."

"It's a lowly job, and it will not pay enough to keep you comfortable."

"We will work together."

"You want to be a teacher."

"Dad, let's trust that this is just a season, and we will still reach our dreams."

Artie smiled. She had made him feel better.

"Let's cook up something nice for tea while we still have a cooker," she laughed loudly.

Isla opened the front door, curtains and windows. Sunshine streamed through the windows and lit up the room. Everything was going to be alright.

*

Artie took up Isla's suggestion and went to see Mr Todd. He explained his position, and Mr Todd told him that Artie would be the oldest apprentice he ever trained, but he would be delighted to have him. He also told Artie that the pay was little, but he would try and give him a few bob more. Mr Todd knew Artie was in need but warned him never to discuss what he received because the other apprentices would be furious. It still remained next to nothing, but it meant the world to Artie.

Isla knew her best chance to find work would be in the fish market. She walked from stall to stall, boat to boat, until she found a job collecting and scrubbing the fish entrails off the floor. Isla arrived home with a big smile and great excitement.

"What is it, lass?" Smiled Artie.

"I've found a job down at the market."

"What will you do down there?" Artie frowned.

"Just a bit of everything," she lied.

Isla's job was the lowest. She wouldn't tell her father. He would chastise himself.

"When do you start?"

"Tomorrow at six o'clock," she beamed.

She was truly delighted to have found work. It was one step out of the mire. Things could only get better.

*

Isla loved her job. She did her work enthusiastically and always had a bright smile. She added sunshine to an otherwise dim environment, and her disposition was contagious. She swept through the market every morning, smiling and greeting everyone she saw. Even the most miserable old people became cheerful when they saw her coming along.

"Good morning lass," shouted Mr Leyton, "how is the day treating you so far?"

"Very good, Leyton. I have no complaints."

"How is your dad doing?" Mr Leyton asked.

"All good, Sir."

"Have you found somewhere to live yet?"

"Yes, and close by as well. It's cosy and warm."

Mr Leyton knew the place that Artie and Isla had moved into. There was nothing charming about it, yet Isla had seen the potential and had managed to make it liveable.

It was fundamentally a small room under a house that stood close to the sea. The door led onto cobble stones, and at spring tide, the water almost reached their doorstep. The first winter in their new abode, the wind had driven the water so high that it flooded the cottage.

Artie and Isla would have none of it, and with the landlord's permission, they devised a way to keep their home dry. The small cast-iron stove ensured that the room was warm, and it didn't take a lot of fuel to heat. They could comfortably afford coal. Artie had rescued two narrow cots from a tip, and they served as beds and seating. They were not rich or even comfortable. In fact, they were very poor.

Isla would bring fish heads home. With a few potatoes and some carrots, she managed to create a wholesome broth. During the annual sardine run, Mr Todd allowed his men to take home food for their families, which saved them a lot of money.

*

Mr Tremaine watched the young woman scrub the fish entrails off the floor. She had caught his eye because her strawberry-blonde hair was the only bright feature in the otherwise dim marketplace. She stood up and gave him a broad smile, which reached her blue eyes. She was dazzlingly beautiful, although that wasn't what made her attractive. It was the sincere joy that radiated from her face. Mr Tremaine stood in a mild stupor watching her, and he must have looked confused because she greeted him.

"Good afternoon, Sir. How may I assist you?"

"Do I seem lost?" he replied.

"Unfortunately, you do, Sir," she replied, smiling politely.

Mr Tremaine couldn't help but beam. She was a woman of good humour. He estimated her age to be approximately twenty and wondered how such a well-spoken young lady was scrubbing putrid, stinking floors. Mr Tremaine asked her an arbitrary question, and she gladly pointed him in the right direction. Another good sign.

Mr Tremaine returned to Victoria Manor, where he served as a butler. The manor house was approximately five miles from St Ives and stood on a cliff overlooking the sea. It was the summer home of Lord Belmont and his family, where they entertained aristocracy, gentry, the rich and the famous. The locals had very little exposure to the inhabitants of the great house, bar competition to sell them goods.

Mr Tremaine went straight to the housekeeper's office, standing at the threshold respectfully.

"Ahem."

She looked up from the journals she was perusing and smiled.

"Hello, Stanley."

"Doreen, I have found somebody I think you should meet."

The housekeeper frowned. Who was it this time?

"It's a young woman down at the fish market. She scrubs up the floors there. I think she would be a worthy investment."

"Why's that?" asked Mrs Pengelly.

"She is doing that dreadful job, and she has a permanent smile on her face."

Mrs Pengelly laughed.

"Stanley, you have always liked pretty girls."

"I didn't say that she was pretty," he objected.

"Is she?"

"Of course, she is," he replied, feeling foolish.

"How will I recognise her?"

"She is the only enthusiastic person in that godforsaken place."

"Right then, Stanley, the next time I go to St Ives, I will find her."

*

One month later, Doreen Pengelly had reason to travel to St Ives. After she had completed her business, she headed towards the fish market. She walked up and down the myriad of stalls and past piles and piles of fish that lay stacked in boxes but had no success finding the girl. Out of desperation, she approached an aged and worn fishwife and said she was looking for a pretty girl with strawberry blonde hair who was always smiling.

The woman looked Mrs Pengelly up and down, then pointed to the pickling factory.

"The weather's bad today. They've gone soft and got her working inside."

"You know who I am talking about?"

"Of course, lovely girl. Hard worker. Never complains. Isla Dickson is her name."

"Thank you, madam," said the housekeeper. "You have been very helpful."

Mrs Pengelly stood in the great doorway that led into the factory. In the distance, she could see a blonde head bobbing up and down. *'That must be her.'* A stern-looking man spotted the trespasser and approached.

"Good afternoon, Sir. I wish to speak to a certain Isla Dickson. I appreciate she is working, but I have important family news I must impart."

The man promptly turned around and cheerily shouted at the top of his lungs.

"Isla, lass, someone to see you!"

A girl came rushing towards them, exuding energy.

"I'll leave you to it, Isla," said the man before returning to his duties.

Mrs Pengelly had no trouble deciding.

"I am offering you a job at Victoria Manor, and I will pay you triple the wages you make here."

Isla's jaw dropped.

"You will begin on Monday. Tell them you need to leave to look after a sick relative. I am sure your shoes will be easy to fill. Many a lass round here can clean a floor."

Isla put down her scrubbing brush and ran to the beach, where her father was busy mending his nets.

"You won't believe what has happened, Pa! I am going to work at Victoria Manor for triple what I get at the market."

"How did this come about," chuckled Artie.

"I don't really know. This woman just appeared and told me to be there on Monday. Seems word must have got round I'm a grafter?"

"Good for you, lass, good for you. Of course, things won't be easy for us even at triple the wage."

"I know, I know, but it will help us more than the pittance at the pickling plant."

Isla did the calculation, the wage wasn't a king's ransom, but in comparison to what she was earning before, it was close. It was going to be a wrench leaving her father behind, but she consoled herself it was for their own good.

10

VICTORIA MANOR

On Monday morning, at six o'clock sharp Isla arrived at the imposing manor house, struggling to carry a trunk containing all her meagre possessions. What she thought was a light load in St Ives weighed a ton when it reached its final destination five miles away.

Mrs Pengelly was taken aback that she had been so punctual at such an early hour, especially considering the distance she had to cover to get there. Isla's conscientiousness made a good first impression upon the housekeeper, and the two of them were off to a good start.

"Now, to confirm your terms of employment. You will receive board and lodgings in one of Lord Belmont's servants' quarters and you will be paid nine shillings a week, a total of £23 9s. Is that agreed?"

"Very much so," said Isla, adding a small curtsey. "Thank you, Ma'am."

"You will have two Sundays off every month. I think you will agree, Lord Belmont is more generous than other employers."

The woman was right. The pay was much better than slaving away at the fish market, and an extra day's leave a month was an exception rather than the rule.

"Now, let's sort out a nice smart uniform for you, make you look the part," announced Mrs Pengelly, as she strode down a long stony-grey corridor peppered with glossy dark brown doors. "Come along, girl. We don't have all day."

She scuttled behind Mrs Pengelly, secretly pinching herself to make sure her good fortune was real. Imagining her father struggling without her nagged at her conscience. Having cared for his beloved daughter, his pride and joy, every day for eight years, he would undoubtedly miss her. Still, her wage was very much needed, and the thought of two Sundays together made her heart a little lighter. When she had her first free moment, she planned to pen a cheery letter to Artie to confirm the good news.

It took Isla a good while to get used to the myriad of rules of the manor. Mrs Pengelly was stern but kind. Sidney Tremaine kept a stiff upper lip as demanded by his master. He had a no-nonsense attitude. Everything had to be perfect for Lord Belmont. His father and mother had been in service, and he understood how unreasonable some of the house rules were, but still enforced them to the letter.

Still, Isla was luckier than many a maid. Both Doreen and Stanley appreciated how exhausting the chores could be and that servants were human. They were far away from their families. They struggled to survive on the little bit they earned after sending the majority of their wage back home. They succumbed to illness. They wanted to marry.

They wanted a life, nothing ostentatious, just some basic home comforts and free time to enjoy simple pleasures and pastimes.

It baffled the mind that most aristocrats, owners of thousands of acres of land, living in mansions, exhibiting their wealth in their magnificent houses and clothing, begrudged their staff leave to visit their parents. The meals were often rationed to basic foodstuffs like porridge, boiled potatoes, and bone broth. They remunerated the desperate with as little as the person would accept, and demanded that they be invisible 'non-persons' at all times. The pantries were full, meat was in abundance, the dogs and horses were fed copious amounts of hay, barley, and molasses in their feed. They retained the services of a vet should an animal become ill. The stablemen boiled up meat to feed the dogs, who had to maintain their energy for the hunt. Horses got new shoes, carts got new wheels, but servants walked miles in agony to and from the market, without considering a cart to transport them. For Lord Belmont, the people who worked at Victoria Manor for their meagre stipend were less important than the livestock, horses, and dogs because they could be replaced for free and had no resale value.

In such a rural county, endless poor people fought for the odd bit of casual labour. In St Ives, the streets were teeming with people lacking the bare necessities to keep them alive: shelter, food, heat, and hope. This situation wasn't unique to St Ives - it was common in all Cornish towns. Even the most moral of men might turn to crime to make ends meet. The worst punishment was meted out on the men who hunted on the royal ground or collected wood for their fires. Many peasants were put in gaol for snaring a rabbit or grouse or collecting kindle. Few aristocrats ventured into the low-lying harbour towns. They preferred to live high above the riffraff and were amused by the scenarios playing out far below. They were so removed from reality that they observed their fellow men like the little handmade models in a diorama.

*

On her first day, Mrs Pengelly sent Isla off to work with another maid, Katy. By the time they reached the top of the servant's staircase, they were best friends. A bit of a newcomer herself, Victoria Manor had been Katy's workplace for eight months.

"I'm a 'tweener," Katy said.

"What on earth's that?" quizzed Isla, smirking.

"I'm always 'tween this and that."

Katy burst into silent giggles, not daring to make a noise. If Lord and Lady Belmont were close, she would get her ears boxed. The aristocracy didn't like happy poor people.

"You will also be a tweener," Katy whispered. "It doesn't pay as well as the best jobs in the household, but at least you aren't stuck in one place all day. They send you wherever you are needed."

"What are the others like?"

"Servants?" Katy whispered.

Isla nodded.

"The housekeeper and butler are very nice people. They really protect us all as much as they can. We all get along, "

"Protect?"

"The family is very difficult. The lady thinks we can read her mind. She never moves her mouth when she speaks."

Katy mimicked the lady's mannerisms and Isla tried not to giggle.

"Just stay out of their way and don't see or say anything. And, er, never look them in the eye."

"But, how do you do that? I've looked at people all my life. It's an instinct I can't just turn on and off."

"Just stare at one of those stuffed animals on the wall. They love stuffed animals, so they do. They are all over the place. I'm surprised that they don't stuff people. Imagine Sir Frances Drake in the corner of Lord Belmont's bedroom."

Isla could imagine it, and this time, she couldn't stifle her laugh.

"Right, enough chat, or Mrs Pengelly will be after us. We must dust Lord Belmont's library. Tilly Proctor is ill. She usually does it. Mrs Pengelly has assigned her to the library because she is a rather frumpy girl, and Lord Belmont will not give her any unnecessary attention."

"What's the worst job in the house?" asked Isla.

"Slops, but things have improved. They have installed water closets that have replaced the crappy commodes."

The pun wasn't lost upon her and Isla burst into giggles again. That soon stopped when she heard creaking footsteps behind them and saw Mr Tremaine approaching.

"That's enough, Katy, Isla. Be on your way. The library won't clean itself. His Lordship is expecting an important visitor and one speck of dust will enrage him."

"Yes, Sir. Sorry, Sir," Katy and Isla chimed.

The two made their way across the large house. Isla was fascinated by the maze of secret servant's corridors that ran parallel to the lavish ones in the manor.

"See that wooden panelling? Well, in this house it's really a system of hidden doors. If I see one of the Belmonts on the horizon, I am to use the closest exit and disappear."

"Oh, and don't shake your feather duster in our corridors when you're done. One of us servants may think that you are a magician vanishing in a puff of smoke," she said with glee.

The talk of magic brought Freya to mind. Isla had not thought of her mother in years.

*

Artie and Isla's little room could have fitted into the library fifty times over. It was the same size as the ballroom that she had scooted past earlier. The walls had shelves that stretched from floor to ceiling.

"How do they reach the top if they want a book?" Isla asked.

"They don't. The only books that are real are those the visitors can reach. The rest are false."

"Stop it, Katy. You're pulling my leg."

"I'm not. Come, let me show you. A lot of trickery goes on in this old place. All this panelling between the book cases hides secret doors, just like the corridors. If you look carefully, you'll spot a peep hole here and there, too."

"My word, why on earth all this secrecy."

"I have often found one of the family eavesdropping on another's conversation."

"No!"

"Yes! And I have also come upon his lordship in compromising situations with women—who were not his wife," she confessed, with raised eyebrows.

"No! You're making this up."

"Not!"

"What did you do when you found him then?"

"Well, I disappeared quietly into the corridor outside, hoping there wouldn't be a brigade of important visitors out there, marching along like the Coldstream Guards."

Isla shook her head and frowned.

"Little Lord Cornwall is always in the servant's corridors," Katy told her.

"Who?"

"Peter Belmont, the lord's son. If anybody in this house is dangerous, he's the worst. Just keep away from him. I don't like him. He is very handsome and oh so smarmy, but there's something unsettling about him."

"Why?" asked Isla.

"It's how he looks at you when you're alone. There have been rumours of him molesting servants and the lady sacking them because they were pregnant, knowing full well that they were her son's nippers."

"What happened to the women?"

"Some died while they were trying to bring the child down early. Others discard the babies after birth and allow them to die. Then again, it is said that the young man has rid himself of his offspring by killing them with his own hands.."

One girl was hanged because they found her child dead in a ditch, but I don't reckon she did it."

"That is horrible."

"Yes, it is. And it's futile to report it to the coppers. Nobody will dare risk their lives."

"Surely, Lady Belmont will chastise her son?"

"The lady and her son are as thick as thieves. Be aware of them, Isla. He may very well be the next Lord Belmont, and he will look after his mother very well if his father dies. The lady will not go about upsetting him, so none of us is safe," Katy explained.

"And these children? Surely they have a claim to the estate?"

"It is impossible to prove who the father is. Many a maid has been ridiculed in court and labelled a prostitute for trying to fight for her bairn's corner."

"This abuse, is this common knowledge to the locals?"

"No. We may not talk out of the house. The townsfolk in Cornwall revere the family, mainly because they fear them. Even if one of us did say something, they will not repeat anything bad about them. The worst is during the hunting season. The house is full of people. Mrs Pengelly does her best by making us work in pairs. It does help. They are cowards. They won't do things in front of witnesses."

Katy leaned in.

"Not even the young house boys are safe during the hunting season."

"But men can go to gaol for that!"

"You've got a lot to learn, girl. The lads who are willing get paid handsomely to shut up."

All this sordid information was overwhelming for such a young woman. Isla went quiet. She had felt attracted to a lot of rugged young men but never fallen in love with any of them. She had never considered giving herself to a man, and she could only guess that many of the young maids who worked in the manor felt the same. They must have plans of finding a husband that they loved, having children and pottering around their tiny, humble homes, happy to keep their financial heads just above water. It was difficult enough eking out a living in Cornwall and 'Little Lord Spoilt Brat' could ruin a young woman's life in a flash.

Katy and Isla took out their dusters and skimmed them along the shelves. They had barely started when the door swung open and Lord Belmont entered, alone. When the maids made to exit through a secret door disguised as a bookshelf, he signalled for them to stop.

"Don't leave. Continue what you were busy with."

At the far end of the room, he sat at his desk in an ornate leather chair, slitting open each envelope of the stack of letters balanced on his creamy white blotting pad. He threw ninety-nine per cent of the pile into the fire.

Some were futile requests for assistance from charities. He was so tired of idle hand wringers begging in writing. Some were invitations. He really wished people would send those to his wife. She usually decided who they would associate with.

Two letters from the House of Lords kept him updated with new bills parliament was about to debate. He shook his head as he read that the opposition was considering pursuing the criminality of incest. That would cause a furore among the aristocracy. How else would they keep the great fortunes if they couldn't bequeath it to a nephew, should his son perish.

The last letter was from a young woman who had been a scullery maid at the manor, explaining that the trinket she had been accused of stealing was actually a gift from his son for services rendered. Lord Belmont received at least one of these letters every month. He wished that the boy would be more discreet, but the woman was happy to accept the gift, knowing it wasn't the young man's property to give away. He was comfortable with her standing trial for her own stupidity. Her letter he tore into the tiniest of pieces and dumped it in an ashtray. He took out a match and set the paper alight. For a second, it created a blaze. Within a few seconds, it disappeared, and only the ashes remained. The girls could only wonder at what had made him so furious.

When he finished with the correspondence, he perused the newspapers that Mr Tremaine had put out for him. Every night, a courier was dispatched to Exeter to St. David's railway station to collect yesterday's evening newspaper and deliver it by six o'clock the following morning, come rain or shine.

"You," Lord Belmont snapped, pointing at Katy.
"Come here."

The girl looked up. All her chatty bravado of earlier left her, as she meekly stood in front of his desk.

"Who's she?" he quizzed, nodding over at Isla.

"She is the new tweener, Sir. I am—"

" Her name, for God's sake! Just get to it."

"Miss Dickson, Sir. Isla."

"Get back to your work," he ordered.

"Yes, Sir."

Lord Belmont sat back in his chair. His eyes were riveted on Isla. She was tall and beautiful, with an unusual grace for a commoner. She was humble, but she held her head high, and her confidence irritated him. *My son had better leave this one alone. I want the honour of bringing her down to earth myself.*

"What did he want?" Isla whispered.

"Your name."

Katy's mood had changed. She grew pensive and polished everything with extra vigour. Now, they worked together in silence.

"Why are you so quiet?" Isla whispered.

"Let's just finish up and get away from here."

Katy was troubled. It was never a good sign when one of the Cornwall toffs showed too much interest in a servant.

"Just be careful of him, stay out of his way."

11

THE TEACHER

Katy and Isla shared a small room under the eaves, and it became their private haven of peace after the long days. Eager to relax after her first day, Isla pulled one of the books from her trunk, climbed into bed, and began to read.

"Can you—?" an astonished Katy blurted out.

"Yes."

Isla was absorbed in the story and hoped that Katy would settle down soon. She was a distraction.

"I can't read," Katy prattled away. Isla looked up at her.

"Why not?"

"My parents were tenant farmers. I went to school for a short time, but the hogs needed feeding, and my ma needed help. My pa died young, and I had four young sisters. There were more important things to do, I suppose."

Katy didn't say it with bitterness. There was a relaxedness about her comment, as if she couldn't get a white dress because it was too expensive, so she chose a blue one.

"Where did you learn to read, Isla?"

"My father insisted that I go to school in St Ives. He wanted me to be a schoolteacher."

"He did?"

"Yes, but then we lost everything, and I had to find work here to help keep us going."

"Can you do numbers?" Katy asked in awe.

"Aye."

Isla was taken aback that Katy had never been to school, and she realised that she had been so privileged that she never considered that others around her were illiterate.

"Will you read to me?" Katy asked.

"Of course," laughed Isla.

That is how their ritual began. Every time Isla went home, she would return with new books. Every night after they had washed, they would climb into their narrow cots, and Isla would read. Katy realised that the stories could take her far beyond Cornwall, and she travelled across the world. The words fed her imagination.

One evening, Isla began to read but didn't reach the end of the first sentence before Katy interrupted her.

"Do you think that I can learn to read?"

"Of course."

"I am not as clever as you are."

"Katy, stop it. I wasn't born 'clever'. Somebody taught me as well. Shall I teach you?"

"Oh, Isla, would you?" Katy trilled.

"Of course, I will. I will teach you to read—and write."

"And—will you teach me to do numbers, Isla? Please?"

"I will teach you everything that I know."

Katy couldn't hide her enthusiasm, and she couldn't stop jabbering for an hour.

"You need only do one thing before we begin learning numbers."

Katy looked at her wide-eyed, terrified that she would be too stupid to fulfil the task.

"Go and gather a bag of pebbles. We'll use them as counters for when we do numbers," Isla told her.

The relief on Katy's face was priceless.

"I can do that!" she squealed. "And if learning numbers is as easy as gathering a bag of pebbles, I will learn very quickly."

Katy fell asleep with a broad smile on her face, and Isla was able to read two chapters of her book in peace.

*

When it came to chores, Isla was a quick learner, and soon she and Katy were given separate tasks to accomplish during the day. It was almost hunting season, and the house was in chaos as an army of new faces dusted rooms that hadn't been given a fettle in months. Mrs Pengelly marched Isla downstairs giving her a thorough briefing about how things needed to work.

"Where did all these people come from, Ma'am?"

"We hire extra help for a few weeks during the hunt, Isla. The lady agrees because we always need assistance with the extra workload. The weekend must be viewed by the guests as the greatest event of the season."

"I see," said Isla, not really understanding what hosting a hunt involved at all.

"Every room must be turned over, not a speck of dust."

She spotted a couple of chaps chatting in the corridor and they got a swift tongue-lashing.

"You men, there. Yes, you two." she chided.
"You're not paid to gossip like washerwomen. Get out your ladders. Every lamp and chandelier must sparkle."

Mrs Pengelly carried on laying down the law in the scullery where the main household staff had been requested to assemble. Those who had served at the manor for many years had heard the same speech year after year, and wished their masters would realise that presenting a perfect event was as prestigious for them as it was for the family. They might not have wealth, but pride in upholding high professional standards was ample reward.

"Cook, you are the most important person in this room. Our guests must be fed well. Have you got enough help?"

The exhausted-looking scullery team nodded as one.

"Excellent. Now, Mr Tremaine would like to speak to you all."

Mrs Pengelly gave the floor to Stanley who spent an hour brushing up on staff etiquette, pulling up anyone who slipped. Meanwhile, outdoors, the head groomsman, gardener, and gamekeeper gave similar lectures to their men.

"Anything to add, Doreen?"

"Yes. Now remember, many guests will bring their own valets and maids. We will welcome them and make them comfortable. They will eat at our table, and we will be generous. In this house, we will leave the politicians, gentry, and aristocracy to squabble. Under the stairs, we are all the same, and I will not tolerate servants being greater snobs than their masters."

Everyone nodded in agreement and had a laugh. Year in and year out, when they saw their peers arrive, they would all be secretly judged like cattle at an auction.

*

The task of cleaning the house was always methodical and well-executed. Mrs Pengelly ran a tight ship. Not wanting to risk an embarrassing mistake, new girl Isla, was dispatched to the colder south wing of the house, where the less popular guests and low-ranking politicians would be accommodated. It wasn't a compliment to be given a suite here, rather a very subtle hint that the occupant would either have to be more accommodating in business or pleasure. In addition, the close proximity of a room to the privy was an indicator that its occupant would not be on the guest list the following year.

Few men refused the Belmont's invitation, but those that did were usually self-made industrialists who didn't rely on their aristocratic connections for favours. Once such invitee who had always snubbed Lord Belmont's invitation was Samuel Hudson, a well-respected philanthropic man with no tolerance for gentry and aristocracy. The Americans and Europeans loved his trail-blazing engineering prowess. If Samuel could have stomached to return the invitation, he would have placed the odious lord opposite the lavatory. But it was a fantasy. To add insult to injury, Hudson's repeated letters of decline always ended with the reminder that he never hunted and didn't support the practice. When it arrived, Lord Belmont crumpled up the letter and flung the ball of paper into the fire. It was amazing why his wife persisted in putting him on the guest list. How naive he was for a powerful man. Lady Belmont had her own agenda— Samuel Hudson was a powerful, good-looking man.

The lord of the manor was in a foul temper. The letter from Samuel had ruined his day. The aristocrat left his library, slamming one door while the other remained comically open. It was a futile, ridiculous gesture of a tantrum.

He took his mind off the snub by admiring all the priceless art hanging on the walls, examples of how the ancient masters had excelled themselves. He puffed out his chest knowing he owned one of the greatest private galleries in Europe.

It was then he remembered the Constable that he wanted to display with pride of place in the hallway. The piece was hanging in one of the bedrooms on the far side of the house. He decided a walk to inspect it would relax him. A work of such significance needed to be in pristine condition. If it fell short, he would instruct Mr. Tremaine and his mob to dust the frame before carrying it down to the hall.

Lord Belmont reached the south wing and made his way down the long corridor lined with lavish chinoiserie silk carpets embroidered with rich peacock blues, greens and gold. What a pity that the Empire had not conquered China yet, he mused. There was such an abundance of wealth to bring home from there. For the last four hundred years, the generals had refused to consider the suggestion. Even during the Opium Wars, they had never been tempted to invade.

Unsure of the precise location in his rabbit-warren of rooms, Lord Belmont began to systematically search one after the other. When he approached the fourth of the fifteen rooms on that floor, a door panel opened, and a maid emerged from the servant's corridor.

The instant that Isla saw Lord Belmont, she stepped back into the passage and quietly shut the door behind her. She was already some distance away from him when he shouted at her.

"You. Stop. Come here this instant."

Isla put down her cleaning basket and walked towards him. He could see her confidence, but also her innocence. Her cap covered her strawberry-blonde hair. Not a strand of golden silk could be seen. If the girl thought it would make her look anonymous and blend in with the other servant girls, she was wrong. He stared at her blue eyes that were lined with pitch-black lashes and dark eyebrows that framed the stunning combination. Then his eyes settled on her perfect unblemished skin, and he followed the curve of her perfect neck until it disappeared under the collar. Lord Belmont was aroused.

"Good morning, Sir."

"Name?"

"Isla, Sir."

"I recall you were in my library."

"Yes, Sir."

"I am looking for a painting, you will assist me in searching for it. There is a Constable in one of these rooms. It is too magnificent to be hidden in this dreary wing of the house."

They stepped into the hallway, and Isla turned right.

"Where are you going?" asked Lord Belmont.

"The Constable is in room eight of this floor, Sir."

"How do you know that?"

Isla ignored the question, and he noted the snub.

"I have dusted the frame, but I have not touched the canvas. The rooms on this side of the house are damp. It is at risk of getting mildew."

Lord Belmont was taken aback by her knowledge but annoyed by her boldness and sour that she had not answered his question. She should have been tongue-tied and her knees shaking. She was a commoner. How dare she display any signs of education. Didn't she know that it was an insult to him? Did she know with whom she was speaking? Evidently, she didn't, and it didn't matter to her one jot. As annoyed as he was, an idea came to mind, an idea that would give him direct control over her. A dark smirk contorted his ogre-like features.

*

Lord Belmont summoned Mr Tremaine to his private study, where he liked to hold court and make and execute his most important decisions.

"Tremaine, the young maid, Isla Dickson."

"Yes, Sir."

"She seems brighter than the others. I have decided that she will be solely dedicated to the care of my art collection. It is her duty to dust and keep a log of the condition that they are in."

"Is that all, Sir?"

"No, Tremaine, instruct Mrs Pengelly to increase her wages by three shillings a week."

"Yes, Sir."

Belmont looked down at his desk then snapped:

"You can go, now."

*

Mr Tremaine went directly to Mrs Pengelly's office. He looked unusually sombre, and instantly the woman knew that something was wrong.

"What has happened, Stanley?"

"He has noticed her, Doreen. He wants Isla to be solely responsible for cleaning the artworks and keeping a log of their condition."

Mrs Pengelly shook her head. She had witnessed Lord Belmont stalking many a young maid, it always began this way, and it always ended badly.

*

Katy tore through the door like a battering ram. She was full of smiles.

"What has happened?" Isla gasped.

"Wee Betsy Trenton in the laundry rooms wants you to teach her to read."

"You are a handful by yourself, Katy," Isla groaned.

"And there are three others."

"Oh no! What have you done?"

"Oh, Isla, this will mean so much to them.

"Alright, Katy, but no more. Where would we fit them?"

This was how the learning circle grew. Late at night, when they were dismissed from duty, Isla's students would gather in the room with her and Katy. Slowly but surely, more and more servants arrived until they were packed into the small area like sardines. For thirty minutes every night, they had a lesson and slowly began to learn the alphabet, and finally, they started to read.

12

THE HUNT AND THE HUNTED

Lord Belmont's guests began to arrive late on Friday afternoon. They rumbled up the driveway in ostentatious cabs, followed by an entourage of servants and nannies to ensure that their masters would have uninterrupted peace for the weekend.

Isla spent the evening assisting her counterparts in making their masters happy. Lord Belmont's staff maintained good humour and went beyond all expectations making everybody welcome. Later, the visiting servants wouldn't stop talking about the generosity of spirit in the kitchens and stables at Victoria Manor.

*

Mr Tremaine rushed into the kitchen so fast that his coattails had a job keeping up with him.

"Mr Peter Belmont has arrived," he shouted above the din of voices.

Mrs Pengelly gave him a look which he couldn't misinterpret. She had no time for the young man. Even as a child, she had disliked his precocious arrogance, and his manners had not improved since attending Oxford.

"Isla, please take the tea tray to Mrs Carter's suite," Mrs Pengelly said. "She is in the north wing, room eighteen."

Isla lifted the heavy tray and took the servant's staircase to the second floor then popped through a panelled door on the left and glided towards room eighteen. Before she could knock on the door, she saw a good-looking young man walking towards her. When he saw Isla struggling with her fragile load, he walked straight towards her and put his arms out to relieve her of the tea tray.

"Let me assist you, my dear," he cooed, oozing charm.

She was reluctant to hand over the tray, but he pulled it away from her, and for fear of spilling, she allowed him to take it.

Young Master Belmont took the opportunity to study her. This was the maid his friends had told him about. They were right. She was worth the bet. The bet as to who would have her first, that is.

Isla knocked on the door of room eighteen. The face of Mrs Carter's maid greeted her. Peter Belmont handed her the tray with a smarmy smile.

"Just as your mistress requested, Miss."

The maid servant looked from Isla to Peter Belmont, confused. Isla gave a slight smile and tilted and moved her eyes ever so slightly towards Belmont, subtly communicating her discomfort. The young woman knew exactly what Isla was trying to convey. Servants could interpret the most subtle cues that they often bordered on mind-reading.

"Thank you. I shall deliver this forthwith."

All Isla wanted to do was get away. She walked briskly towards the servant's exit, but Peter Belmont persisted at keeping at her heel.

"What is your name," he prodded.

Isla didn't answer, panicked by his close proximity to her.

"Has the cat got your tongue?"

Isla opened the door to let herself into the service corridor. Instead of him leaving her be, he followed her. Isla grabbed the front of her long skirt and raised it a little as she began to walk faster.

This time he didn't follow. He stood, rocking on his heels, with his hands in his pockets and watched her go.

"Next time, you won't get away that easily."

*

The following morning, Peter Belmont proceeded to play a game of cat and mouse with Isla until she was terrified. Even though it was long before dawn, the house was abuzz with riders getting ready for the hunt.

Peter ensured that he was in every corridor or on every staircase when Isla was alone. He had grown up in the manor and had played in all the secret passages and corridors in the ancient house. He knew it far better than she ever would. In those few hours he terrorised her to such an extent that she was filled with anxiety every time she turned a corner.

Eventually, he cornered her on the second floor. He pushed himself so close to her that she was backed up against the wall, unable to escape.

"You can't get away from me, Isla," he cooed at her in a sing-song voice, "I will find you wherever you hide."

He moved back a little to view her bosom. Luckily, Isla happened to be near room eighteen. She shoved Peter hard in the middle of his chest. Off balance, he took a few steps back, then she darted out of his clutches and knocked on Mrs Carter's door.

"What's all this racket? My mistress has a headache and is having a lie down," muttered the maid when she saw Isla.

"Mrs Pengelly asked if I could show you the laundry?"

She looked past Isla's shoulder and saw Peter Belmont. Isla's eyes were pleading for Mrs Carter's maid to agree. Mercifully, she left her mistress's room and joined Isla. As Peter Belmont passed them, he was whistling to himself.

Isla couldn't find Mr Tremaine or Mrs Pengelly. Katy was working in the south wing, so the poor girl didn't know who else she could talk to about being harassed.

Isla felt too guilty to send the visiting maid back to her mistress with Peter Belmont prowling about. With trepidation they had to venture back into the terrifying maze as if they were Theseus facing the Minotaur.

"Thank you. You saved me, and I don't even know your name."

The maid smiled.

"I can mention this to Mrs Carter. She will do something about it. She is an American heiress. They are not like the English."

"No. Please don't. I am sure it will cause too much trouble. The Belmonts are very strict and band together when threatened. "

The maid nodded, understanding only too well what Isla meant.

Isla felt more relaxed after speaking to someone, but the moment the maid closed the door behind her, Isla heard a whistle. She spun around and saw Peter at the end of the passage. She turned and ran, but when she reached the top of the grand gilded staircase that descended into the vast hallway below, she stopped. Below, she saw a throng of red coats. All the riders had gathered in the great hallway ready to receive their orders from the Master of the Hunt.

Isla knew that she couldn't rush down the staircase and disrupt the announcements. Worse, she should not even be on the staircase.

Young Belmont was dressed in his riding gear now. He didn't increase his pace as he walked towards her. He was stalking her patiently, like a cat who had all the time in the world. She looked at Peter Belmont, and then she looked down into the foyer.

"If you go down there, you will be in a lot of trouble, Isla."

He was so close to her that she could feel his breath against her skin. The hairs on the back of her neck stood up.

"Just stand still. You don't have to be afraid of me," he laughed softly in her ear.

Isla was snared like a rabbit. She couldn't run down the stairs. She couldn't use the servant's staircase. She couldn't move an inch.

"I hope you are still a virgin, Isla."

Isla gulped. She wanted to cry. She felt adrenaline surge through her body, and her heart began to race.

"My friends and I have a little bet on you," he giggled. "The first one who has you will get a free round at the Bullingdon Club at Oxford."

Isla began to shake.

"But we must be able to prove that we were with you. We agreed that we would tear a piece of lace off your underwear."

Peter Belmont's lips touched her ear, and she felt a hollow sensation in the pit of her stomach.

"It would be so funny if we all produced a piece of lace, wouldn't it?"

He rested his hand on her hip.

"Come, Isla. Come with me. I want to see the lace on your underwear so that I can tell my friends what to expect."

Isla burst into tears. He was a pig, an absolute pig, and she was terrified.

If she had the choice of being raped by Peter Belmont or losing her job, she was prepared to lose her job. The rogue thought Isla would be too terrified to run away from him, and he was taken aback when she bolted forward and tore down the staircase. Thankfully, Lord Belmont had just finished his speech, and all the guests were beginning to leave the main house for the stables. As she reached the ground floor, Peter watched Isla scramble past the guests and make towards the kitchen. He was having so much fun with the new maid. It wasn't the first time he had played this game. The only thing that made it different this time was that she was achingly beautiful.

Just as he was about to make his descent, he saw his father at the edge of the room. Lord Belmont had seen Isla tearing down the staircase, and he was livid. He gazed up to see what had startled her and saw his son Peter looking down. Isla had to pass Lord Belmont to reach the kitchen door, but just before she could retreat below stairs, he stepped forward and grabbed her by the arm, bent down, and whispered something in her ear.

"Get into my study," he ordered.

Lord Belmont sounded ruthless.

*

By the time the lord reached his study, Isla's face was tear-streaked, and she was gasping for air.

"What happened?" Belmont demanded.

"Nothing, Sir. I will be fine. I saw a very big spider, and I was terrified."

"You are not the type of girl who is frightened by spiders."

He gave Isla his handkerchief.

"Is it my son?"

Isla couldn't answer him.

"Damn it," cursed Lord Belmont so loudly that she jumped. "Was it him?"

Isla nodded.

"Get out," he shouted at her, "Get out and don't let me see you here again."

*

Lord Belmont took a casual stroll through the reception rooms, eager to find his son. It was a case of 'like grandfather, like father, like son'. The love of violating young things weaker than themselves was the Belmont legacy. It was like the mathematical expression of pi. It would continue on infinitely.

He reached the great doors that led onto the balcony. He saw his boy standing with his Oxford friends, waiting for the grooms to bring their horses. The young men were all decent, brilliant, privileged, like-minded and bored.

"Oh, hello, Father."

"Peter, my boy," greeted Lord Belmont.

They began a conversation, then slowly they descended the worn old limestone steps together. They reached the pristine garden that his wife was so proud of, the grass of which would be trampled to bits by the time the day was through. The riders were enjoying a light snack of scotch eggs and sherry before they left. Lord Belmont and his son reached a small gazebo, in full view of the house but still reasonably private, given the rows of hydrangeas around it. He had been so sick of his wife talking about the damned things. Now, he was glad that she had planted them.

"Stay away from the maid."

"Which one?" chuckled Peter loudly. He was
rather tiddly due to the sherry.

"The one that you have been terrorising," said his
father.

"Why now, father? The young maids have always
been fair game. You have always joked that it is
one of the master's rights."

"You are not the master of this house yet, Peter."

Peter didn't know how to retaliate. His father had never
spoken to him like this before. The condescending tone
threw him, and, puzzlingly, he became more confused the
more information his father divulged.

"I am thinking of offering your skills to a little
firm in Hong Kong," Lord Belmont said calmly.

"Why?

He could think of no worse place to land up than in Hong
Kong. It was a colony. He didn't want to end up being run
around on rickshaws, having palm fronds waved over his
head and sailing down rivers in a bloody sampan. The
whole idea was abominable. If his father had suggested
Boston, or better yet, New York City, he would agree right
there and then.

Peter heard his father answer him.

"Because I paid for the fine qualifications you
have received at Oxford, and serving her Majesty

would be an excellent way to show me your gratitude."

The sherry was no longer working as well as it had. Peter's puffed-up demeanour was evolving into misery, aggravated by the spinning sensation in his head. He knew that his father's words were an indirect warning for him to behave himself or be exiled.

"I shall not pursue the young woman any longer, Father."

"I am glad to hear that Peter. I personally don't enjoy Hong Kong that much. It is the heat, the food, and the smell. Not for me. But perhaps the women may be worth the trip."

Peter was left confused. In one breath, his father was chastising him over his treatment of a maid. In the other breath, his father was suggesting that he broaden his horizons and seek an oriental experience.

"I think I will treat you chaps to a little place in London's East End. There is something very special about oriental women."

Lord Belmont turned around and sauntered across the perfectly manicured lawn back to the hunters. The air was crisp. It was autumn. The hunt would start within minutes. He couldn't wait. As long as everybody knew that he was Master of the Hunt, his son was stupid. Did he really think that his father had not noticed the girl? Lord Belmont had been hunting since he was as young as Peter. He wasn't only referring to foxes.

*

Lord Belmont saw Mr Tremaine and signalled for him to come over. Mr Tremaine crossed the busy driveway to where Lord Belmont stood, ready to mount his horse.

"I am worried about young Isla," Lord Belmont explained.

"Yes, Sir, why is that Sir?" Mr Tremaine asked.

"She has worked very hard to have the art presentable for this weekend."

"Yes, Sir, the job suits her very well," answered Mr Tremaine, who wondered where the conversation was leading. Surely there were more important things to do than discuss a staff member in the precious moments before a fox hunt.

"When last did she have time off?"

"Three Sundays ago, Sir."

"Very well, Tremaine, she may take leave from Sunday night and return on Wednesday morning."

"I do not mean to contradict you, Sir, this is the busiest weekend in our calendar, and next week we will be busy returning the house to normal."

"Do as I tell you, Tremaine, pass my orders to Mrs Pengelly."

"Whips cracked, and there was the sound of dogs yelping. Horseshoes clipped on cobble while riders sat upright in their saddles. The red coats were bright and fresh, collars were starched to perfection, and the bows tied either behind or on top of riding hats. In the cold morning, twinkling round and square gold buttons indicated the riders' levels of experience, roles and duties. They were as well polished and obvious as medals earned for bravery. The heat radiated from the mouths and bodies of horse, hound and rider, embalming them in a white aura of mist. They looked ghostly and mythical in the weak sunrise. The bugle sounded, and the hounds raced forward, looking for the scent of a fox. Within minutes they found something. The sound of fifty galloping horses down the turf was exhilarating, as the riders controlled the powerful beasts that made the earth tremble.

"Thank God for that," remarked Mr Tremaine.

"Yes, it is a relief to get them all out of here, but they will be back."

"We have rooms full of spoilt wives to satisfy," smiled Mrs Pengelly, "our job is hardly over."

"Doreen, Lord Belmont insists you give Isla leave from Sunday night."

Mrs Pengelly was perplexed.

"Stanley, did you tell him that we need every pair of hands that we can get?"

"Of course, I did, but he told me that it was non-negotiable."

"I am not happy with the situation here, Stanley. Isla seems to be in a terrible state," Mrs Pengelly shook her head. "She was all over the place this morning. I could get nothing out of her. Then she appeared with Tilly, the American woman's maid, muttering something about the laundry."

"Do you think it has anything to do with Peter?" asked Mr Tremaine.

"Of course, he is a monster."

"Do you think that his father has got wind of his intentions for Isla? I mean, Lord Belmont has a lot of respect for the job Isla is doing. Surely he doesn't want to lose her."

"Don't be naïve, Stanley, never trust any of the aristocracy when they display generosity. There is always an ulterior motive."

13

TRAPPED

"Tomorrow?" exclaimed Katy.

Isla nodded.

"Well, there you go. The master has developed a soft spot for you."

Isla felt guilty. Everybody worked hard. She didn't understand why she was singled out.

"It feels awkward," she told Katy, "it is the busiest weekend of the year, and I am sent home."

"Perhaps Lord Belmont believes that he is protecting you from his pig of a son." Katy was outraged by Peter Belmont's behaviour when Isla told her of his threats.

"I must be honest, I am glad to be going. Peter Belmont frightened me a great deal."

"Go off and enjoy two days with your Pa" Katy told her. "It will be a lovely surprise for him."

*

It was six o'clock in the evening when she left the manor. The weather had been fine for the whole weekend, but by Sunday evening, the wind was blowing hard, and cold, damp air was pushing in from the coast, creating a fog so dense it was difficult to see through.

Isla didn't take very much with her. She would only be gone for two days. It was a quick walk to St Ives. She would reach the town within two hours, if not less.

"Go on now, lass, don't stop for anyone or anything. Enjoy your time off and send my regards to your father," instructed Mrs Pengelly.

"Thank you," said Isla. Excitement had settled over her, and she was full of smiles.

"Get away now," said Mr Tremaine, "time waits for no lady," he teased.

*

Isla left the manor by way of a side entrance. She walked into the gale. Her coat served little purpose as the wind managed to blow up the hem of her dress. Her bonnet wouldn't stay put, and the ends of her scarf whipped around her face and stung her rosy chapped cheeks. She was in two minds whether to take a shortcut through the copse. The road was well established through the wooded area and about half a mile long. Many people trampled their way along it, so there was no fear of getting lost.

Isla could only see a few yards ahead of her because of the mist. She was better sheltered by the wind and could move faster. She could vaguely make out the flat ribbon of the road in front of her.

Above the din of the forest, she heard the neigh of a horse and then hooves. The animal wasn't moving fast, hardly a trot. Isla stepped to one side, afraid that the rider wouldn't see her and that he would ride over her.

She kept moving, but carefully now. The horseman kept the same pace. If he passed her, she could relax. She looked behind her and saw the opaque glow of a lamp. Isla grew a little scared and stepped off the road far enough to be hidden by the foliage. From her position, she watched as the horseman passed by. She couldn't identify the rider in the dark. He wore dark oilskins, not unusual on a night like that. It was impossible to see his face. Isla wondered if she had made the right decision choosing the route through the trees. By now, she was in the middle of the woods, and turning around would mean lengthening her journey by hours. Isla stepped back onto the road and continued through the mist and darkness.

Isla continued for another ten minutes, then she heard the horse again. A few paces later, she saw the lamp standing in the middle of the road.

Isla stopped at the lamp.

"Hello," she called, "are you lost? Can I help you?"

There was no reply.

"Hello, are you hurt? Can I help you?"

Still, there was no reply. Isla couldn't see anything. She was blinded by the glow of the light as it bounced off the fog. When there was no response to her calling, she stepped around the lamp, took a few steps further and saw the silhouette of a man in the dim shadows of the lamp.

The ghostly apparition approached her silently. His face was covered by a black mask called a balaclava. He had removed his coat, and he loomed over her.

Isla took two steps back.

"Can I help you? Are you hurt?"

The person didn't reply.

Isla instantly regretted taking a shortcut through the copse. She should have stayed on the main road, she realised that she had made a terrible mistake. She knew that she was in danger.

Isla tried to move around the man, but he wouldn't budge. As quick as a whip, he grabbed her. Isla screamed, but there was nobody to help. She fought back with all her might, but the stranger was far stronger than her.

She screamed again, and this time the man slapped her, and she fell to the ground. He reached out and grabbed her neck, lifting her onto her feet. She squinted down at his hands. There was a black birthmark on the inside of his wrist. Isla twisted her head and bit him. Although he made no sound, he lost his temper. This time he hit her with a fist. She flew through the air and landed on her back, cracking her head against the trunk of a tree.

Her assailant took advantage of her dazed condition. He stood in front of her and unbuttoned his trousers. Isla began to scream when she realised his intentions. He ripped her coat apart, then lifted her dress, and thrust himself inside of her until he was satisfied. The man was insatiable. When she thought he was done with her, she began to crawl into the bushes, but he wasn't finished. He kicked her in the belly, and she collapsed. This time he took her like an animal. Then, he pulled up his trousers and walked into the dark.

Besides the frightful pain, Isla was terrified to move. She pulled her coat closer around her, but she couldn't button it. They had all been ripped off. She began to shake, not as when she was cold, but violent shudders. She crawled towards the road. It was pitch dark. The rider was gone.

Isla collapsed into the road. She tried to stand, but her body was ripped to shreds. As she lay in the dark, she didn't care if she lived or died. She couldn't imagine what her life would be like after this.

*

It was first light when the buggy stopped next to Isla. At first, Trenton thought that it was a branch that had broken off in wind until he realised that it was a person. He jumped to the ground, and slowly approached the ragged heap, and immediately recognised Isla, the young lass who worked in the house. Since he was the youngest footman at the manor, his weekly duty drive to St Ives every Monday morning was to collect the newspapers that arrived from London for Lord Belmont.

Trenton dropped to his knees next to Isla. He saw Isla's blood-soaked bloomers and pulled down her dress, riding above her hips. Trenton didn't know what to do. The young man had never witnessed such a terrible scene. He was paralysed with horror.

Trenton just looked at Isla for a few minutes, trying to decide whether to simply drive around her and forget that he had ever been there or help the girl.

Isla's eyes flickered. She opened them slightly, then they closed. She was in a dreadful mess.

"Who did this?" Trenton asked.

Isla didn't have the will to respond.

"Let's try and get you into the buggy and take you back to the house."

"No."

"Did someone from the house do this to you?"

"Don't know."

"I must do something with you. Where were you going?"

"Shouldna taken this road."

Trenton had sisters. He got tears in his eyes, realising that Isla believed the attack was her own fault.

"Can I take you somewhere?"

"Home."

"St Ives?"

"Mmm."

When Trenton tried to lift her, she screamed, clutching her chest. Two of her ribs were broken when she was kicked.

"The drive will be bumpy," Trenton warned her, "I should take you to Mrs Pengelly."

"No," Isla grunted through her teeth, "take me home."

*

Trenton made Isla as comfortable as he could. He lay her on the seat and covered her with his coat. Her head rested on his lap.

'Gods above,' he thought to himself, 'if she dies, there will be a lot of questions to answer.'

He couldn't drive fast, every bump was a torment for Isla, and his trip took him two hours longer than usual. Lord Belmont would be murderous when he got back. He would be lucky if he still had a job.

'Bugger that too', he told himself.

Working for Lord Belmont had long since lost its charm. Truth be told, Cornwall had lost its charm. He had saved a lot of money, and when he had enough, he would book a passage on a mail ship and sail to wherever the wind blew him.

*

Trenton steered the buggy down the hill and into the High Street. The harbour was teeming with people,

Isla was shielded under the buggy's canopy. Nobody could see her.

"Isla, we are in St Ives. Where must I take you?" Trenton asked gently.

When she didn't answer him, Trenton looked around for the closest bobby.

*

Constable Andrews pulled the coat away from Isla's face and looked at her. She had grown up in front of his eyes, but he didn't recognise her.

"What happened here?" He looked at Trenton accusingly.

"I knew this would bring trouble," mumbled Trenton.

"We both work for Lord Belmont. I was on my way here when I found her lying in the woods. She refused to be taken back to Victoria Manor. She wanted to come here."

"How bad off is she?" asked the constable.

"It is terrible. She needs a doctor."

"There is a small hospital in Lucas Street, can you please take her. I will meet you there."

The officer could see that there would be no space for all of them in the buggy.

*

Constable Andrews took charge of the situation and sent two orderlies out to the buggy. They put Isla onto the stretcher as carefully as they could. The matron took one look at Isla and put her in a private room.

Matron Somers shook her head. Abuse against women was almost a national sport, and the cases increased every month. She grimaced as she looked at the innocent girl. Who would do such a thing?

"Do you know her, Matron?" asked Constable Andrews.

"Yes," the Matron nodded sadly, "her name is Isla Dickson, Artie Dickson's daughter."

The Constable's eyes widened with shock.

"Is this her? Oh, dear God, she is in a frightful way."

By now, a pack of nurses surrounded Isla. They slowly cut off her shredded clothes. As they reached her undergarments, they saw that they were drenched with blood."

"Fetch Dr Jennings," shouted the Nursing Sister.

A young staff nurse flew out of the ward, into the street, and up the hill. She reached the doctor's surgery panting.

"Something terrible has happened, doctor," she panted. "You must come immediately."

Dr Jennings looked at Nurse Gresham and shook his head. The young woman was over dramatic, and it irritated him.

He put on his coat and hat, then picked up his medical bag. He walked down the hill towards the hospital at an even pace and watched Nurse Gresham tearing towards the hospital as though somebody was dying.

The Matron was a few decades older than the doctor, and it gave her rank over him.

"Hurry up, Simon, what's this dawdling along. I am sure Nurse Gresham told you that this case is critical."

Dr Simon Jennings was instantly alert. He was seldom chastised by the matron. The urgency of the matter had been made obvious by her tone, and he followed her, close at heel.

*

Young Dr Jennings had been practising medicine for ten years. He lifted the sheet that covered Isla. He looked down at her and got tears in his eyes. He swallowed hard and blinked them back. Simon Jennings shook his head slowly. He had never seen a case like this before. It was the most savage attack on a woman he had ever seen.

14

INDIFFERENCE

Isla refused to divulge what had happened to her. All she continued to say was that she didn't remember anything. Half the lie was an effort to forget the experience. The other half was to save Artie Dickson the pain of knowing what a man had done to his daughter. Artie would have blamed himself. After all, he had bankrupted them, and Isla had been forced to find a job. Isla swore the hospital to secrecy and begged the matron to contain any gossip.

Artie was very surprised when he received the news that Isla was at the little hospital.

"A bit of an accident," answered Nurse Gresham when Artie asked what had happened to Isla.

Isla was her bright and breezy self when she saw Artie enter the ward.

"You look like you were in a bar fight, lass!" Artie Dickson exclaimed when he saw her.

"More like a collision with a horse on a dark, misty road," she smiled weakly.

"Now, you listen to me, my girl, you are coming home when you feel better, and I will nurse you to perfect health."

Isla smiled at her father. He had so much faith in human nature.

"I'm coming along well with the nets. I have got a raise as well. I do other odds and ends here and there. You have a lot of time to recuperate before you think of work again. And you don't need to work at that big house anymore. No more working so far away, I can see that you don't know how to look after yourself," Artie laughed good-naturedly.

"I promise that I will stay here," smiled Isla. "You will be the best nurse in the world."

*

Matron Somers watched the tender exchange between father and daughter. She could see that they meant the world to each other, yet she was concerned that Isla was prepared to keep the truth a secret from the very person who would love and protect her the most.

When Artie left, Matron Somers went to see Isla.

"Your father is a grown man, Isla. You can tell him what happened. You don't have to be ashamed."

"Matron, you live in a world where you witness this regularly. My father would never dream of doing this to a woman. Nurses and doctors can expand on these issues, but I just want it to go away."

"Isla, are you being truthful when you deny knowing the perpetrator of this crime."

She had been so brave for her father, but she felt sad and empty, and tears rolled down her cheeks.

"Please don't doubt me, Matron. If I knew who it was, I would tell you."

Matron Somers squeezed Isla's hand. Dr Jennings had said that it would be some weeks before Isla's ribs would knit and some time before she healed internally.

"She may not walk until I say so," Dr Jennings ordered, "we cannot risk internal bleeding. I am doing everything that I can to save her female organs. It is a miracle that she didn't bleed to death."

*

Trenton returned to Victoria Manor very late on Monday afternoon. He put the newspapers on the table at the same time that Mr Tremaine came into the kitchen.

"By Gods, Trenton. What has taken you so long? Lord Belmont is behaving like a mad man, something about the Bank of England. For God's sake, you had better have a good explanation for this," ranted the butler.

Mrs Pengelly heard the furore and flew out of her office to hush the noise.

"I am sure they can hear you both in the library, drop your tone immediately, and discuss this matter like grown men."

"Why are you so late? Where have you been?" Mr Tremaine asked in a lowered voice.

"I have a very good explanation if you care to listen," Trenton retaliated.

Mrs Pengelly watched the charged exchange. She understood Mr Tremaine's ire, but young Trenton was behaving out of character. He looked angry, on the brink of exploding.

"Go ahead, I hope that Lord Belmont is satisfied with your excuse."

"I don't think he would be, since when is he ever satisfied? I don't give a fig whether he is satisfied or not. He can shove his wretched newspapers."

A hush fell over the conversation, and the three adults looked at each other astounded.

"What on earth has happened, Trenton? Tell us." Mrs Pengelly coaxed him kindly.

Young Trenton pulled out a chair and sat down. His eyes filled with tears, and he started to cry.

"Isla," he whispered, "I was on my way to St Ives through the woods. I found her. Someone had done the most terrible things to her. I couldn't leave her there. I had to take her to the hospital in St Ives."

Mr Tremaine crumpled onto a chair. Mrs Pengelly put her hand to her mouth and began to pace the kitchen. She was dumbfounded.

Trenton found his second breath and stood up.

"Who done it to her?" Mrs Pengelly asked Trenton.

"She didn't know, and if you saw the state she was in, you would understand why. All I want to say is that if I ever found out who the rotter was who did it to her, I will be happy to crush his skull under my horse's hooves."

Mr Tremaine couldn't believe that this well-mannered, reasonable man had lost all sense of tact. What he had witnessed must have been horrific.

"Will she live?" asked Mrs Pengelly.

"I hope so, Ma'am, I really hope so."

"I am sure that when you explain this to Lord Belmont, he will understand," Mr Tremaine was desperate to save the young Trenton's job.

"I'm not explaining anything to him, Sir. It wouldn't surprise me if he or his son has something to do with this. Little Master Belmont is infamous for the way he treats young women, some of them still children."

"That is dangerous talk, Trenton. We are trying to save your job, not protect anybody else."

Trenton nodded in understanding.

"Thank you for your kindness. Mr Tremaine, I am leaving without giving any notice and I am leaving tonight. I know the evil in this house, and I don't want to be anywhere near here. Whoever did this to that young lady is a savage. If you do not allow me to leave this moment, I will surely tell Lord Belmont to shove the London Newspapers up his aristocratic arse."

"Mmm," Mr Tremain cleared his throat while Mrs Pengelly stared out of the window.

"Very good young Trenton, it has been a pleasure working with you," the butler shook Trenton's hand.

"You are a fine and honourable young man, Trenton" Mrs Pengelly said with a smile. "Be off with you, Mr Tremaine and I will see things straight with Lord Belmont."

*

Both Mrs Pengelly and Mr Tremaine were pensive. They sipped their tea slowly, trying to make sense of what they had just heard.

"I knew that it was too good to be true," Mrs Pengelly was the first to speak.

"We don't know who it is yet, Doreen."

"It is somebody from this house, or perhaps more than one."

Stanley Tremaine didn't say anything. The idea was unimaginable.

"I know that Peter had managed to terrify her. Katy let it slip."

Mr Tremaine felt a cloak of despondency settle over him. He knew that he would have to broach the subject with Lord Belmont. He found it distasteful to have to tell his debauched employer about the incident, particularly because Lord Belmont, Peter Belmont, or his little Oxford friends were likely to have committed the crime.

*

Lord Belmont reclined in his overstuffed leather chair and stared at Mr Tremaine. The man was smoking a cigar, and the air was a haze of smoke.

"Why are you telling me the woes of a maid, Tremaine?"

Stanley Tremaine stifled his temper.

"She took care of your art collection, Sir. I assumed it would be important to you."

"So, someone found her in the woods. Are there any more details? What injuries did she have?

Did she continue on her walk to St Ives? These peasant types are quite resilient."

"No, Sir, she couldn't walk."

"Fellow must have done a fine job then," Lord Belmont remarked callously.

Mr Tremaine was filled with revulsion for the swine.

"Thank you for informing me, Tremaine. Please ask Mrs Pengelly to interview another person, she will work for me as did the other little one. I have already forgotten her name."

The butler nodded. He couldn't trust himself to speak.

"Oh, yes, Tremaine. Tell Mrs Pengelly that she must be pretty. I like taking care of these pretty little things."

15

THE IMPOSSIBLE REALITY

Isla remained in hospital for weeks. Katy came to visit Isla when she could, and she always reported back to Mrs Pengelly that Isla was doing very well and in fine spirits. Little did Katy realise that the instant she closed the door behind her, Isla sank into her pillows, anxious and depressed. Isla had mastered putting on a fine face for the world to see, but inside she was riddled with guilt and turmoil. She had brought it upon herself. She should not have taken the shortcut through the woods. If, if, if. The thoughts didn't stop.

Dr Jennings considered giving her Laudanum, but Matron Somers threw such a tantrum when he suggested it, that he discarded the idea.

"Dr Jennings, do you know that laudanum will do more harm than good. When did you last read a medical journal?" She demanded of him.

"I am the doctor, Matron, and you are a bully. You will take my orders."

"Not in my hospital," She stamped her foot.

"Matron, that is enough," said the young Doctor, authority in his voice.

"Simon, I watched you grow up, walked past my house every morning up to the schoolhouse. Now you want to stand in front of me and tell me to listen. Who do you think you are?"

Every day, young Dr Simon Jennings regretted his decision to practise medicine in his hometown of St Ives. The old folk remembered him as a child, and the younger folk remembered him as a playmate. These intimate relationships prevented him from exerting his authority over them as patients. Every consultation ended in a debate, refusal, argument, or near brawl. He was seriously contemplating moving to another town. Now he had to contend with Matron Somers.

"Matron, you must understand that I have studied medicine, and I am the authority, not you."

"If you give that girl laudanum, she will walk around in a daze for the rest of her life. No! Find another way to help her. This is not an opium den."

"I don't know if there is another solution, Matron. I am not worried about the physical wounds, but the mental ones."

"Don't you dare suggest an asylum, Simon?"

"Nobody is talking about an asylum, Matron Somers, but I predict that things will become far worse before they get better."

"You are such a negative person," the Matron accused him.

"I beg to differ, and I cannot emphasize this more. Isla is cocooned in the safety of the hospital. When she leaves, she will be alone. She will have a lot of time to think about what happened to her, and she will have no kind nurses to make her feel better. This is a sensitive situation, matron, trust me."

"How can you be so sure, Simon?" demanded Somers.

"I am a doctor, Matron, and I read medical journals."

"Then why did you make that stupid suggestion regarding the laudanum?"

Simon Jennings shook his head and walked towards the door. He couldn't win. He had read somewhere that they needed doctors in Australia. He loved the idea of working with convicts. It would be heaven compared to what he was suffering now.

*

Dr Jennings was satisfied with Isla's physical progress, and he promised that he would release her in a few days if she promised to rest at home. Instead of Isla being elated, she was afraid.

The nurses had been professional, and the extent and category of Isla's wounds had remained private. The sum total of information the villagers had on Isla's condition was what they could see. She had been trampled by a horse. She had broken ribs, cracked her head, bruised her chops and damaged her legs. Everything else was confidential.

Isla was terrified that people would find out the truth. She would become the talk of the town. She was afraid of being left alone in the little room her father rented, yet she also didn't want to see people.

She loved her father, but she found it difficult to be endlessly cheerful in front of him.

Mostly she wondered if she could have children. She wondered what the future was for women who couldn't bear a child. All families seemed to have an aunt somewhere who was single and childless, the old maid of the family. Was that her destiny? Her thoughts travelled to teaching. Now she understood why so many single old women remained teachers. She didn't want to think about love and romance. She was revolted by the damage a man could cause a woman with his body. Her thoughts were a messy bungle of fears and questions. She didn't bother to travel through her psyche in search of hope. She was convinced that there was no hope left for her.

*

Dr Jennings listened to Isla's chest, first the front and then the back. He studied the whites of her eyes and then graduated to a physical exam. The examination was intimate, and Dr Jennings was nervous given the nature of Isla's experience.

He pressed down on her abdomen gently, identifying each organ. He checked that they were not swollen and that there were unusual nodules or lumps. His hands moved towards her navel, and he felt her colon, then he moved a little lower. Her lower belly felt a little hard. He gently pressed down his fingers and found the edge of what seemed like a hard little orb.

Dr Jennings got such a fright that he jerked upright and knocked a bottle of medicine flying. He tore out of the ward and charged down the hallway. He didn't bother to knock on the matron's door. He just barged in.

The cook was busy discussing meals with the Matron.

"Get out. Hurry up. Get out!"

The cook escaped the room in a huff, and Matron Somers looked at him in wonderment.

Simon didn't give the matron a moment to talk.

"She's pregnant, I am telling you, she is pregnant."

"Who?" Matron Somers was confused.

"Isla, Isla Dickson is pregnant."

"Are you sure?"

Simon finally lost his sense of humour.

"Of course, I'm bloody sure."

"How can it be? She had the most horrendous injuries?"

"I would like to think of her as a modern-day Mary, but not just any old person is chosen for that job. I don't believe in wind pollination. Do you have any better ideas?"

"No, I don't. This is a disaster for her."

Dr Simon Jennings shook his head in awe.

"Can you do something about this, Simon? Surely you can terminate it."

"How dare you even suggest that as a solution, Matron. I am a doctor, I save lives, I have said an oath. I am not an abortionist. Don't ever ask me that question again."

Matron Somers was developing some respect for Dr Jennings. He was no longer the bumbling young doctor but a man of morals and ethics. She felt ashamed of herself.

"Must I tell her?" She asked.

Simon shook his head slowly.

"No, Matron, but thank you for the offering. I am
her physician, and it is my responsibility to give
her the news."

There was no argument. Dr Simon Jennings knew what he
was doing.

*

Dr Jennings looked down at Isla. All the bruises were gone,
and the scars had healed. Her eyes still looked sad and tired.
He wished he had better news for her.

Isla saw how he was looking at her and immediately knew
that something was wrong.

"There is no easy way to tell you this, Isla, but you
are pregnant. You are going to have a baby."

Isla looked at him bewildered, searching his face to
determine if he was joking with her. Dr Jennings was
shaking his head slowly. His hands were in his pockets, and
he began to pace.

"No!" Isla cried out.

"I am sorry."

"I don't want it," she screamed at him, "I don't
want it, cut it out of me!" Isla was hysterical.

"There are people who can do that, Isla, but not
me."

Then Isla said something that would haunt him for the rest
of his life.

"Please, doctor, help me."

It was the worst day of Simon Jennings's career, his most vulnerable patient was begging for help, and he didn't know what to do.

*

Artie had gone out of his way to make the dwelling feel welcoming and went as far as to find flowers to decorate the table. Isla had repaired well, but the inner glow of joy that had so differentiated her from others had been extinguished in one brutal night.

"I will make that, Pa. I need some practice," Isla
smiled at her father, trying to cushion him for
what was to come.

There was a knock at the door, and Artie opened it. Dr Jennings stood on the steps looking grave.

"Mind if I come in, Artie?"

"Not at all, lad. My, my, you do begin house calls
soon after you send your patient home," Artie
laughed loudly.

Simon smiled at him, then looked over at Isla, and gave her a small nod.

"Can I pour you tea?" Isla asked the doctor.

"Thank you."

"Come, come, sit down," Artie hustled the doctor
into a chair, "sit down, Isla, this is our first visitor

since you have arrived home, we must celebrate, I have some biscuits somewhere," Artie wouldn't stop talking.

"Sit down, Pa," Isla told him firmly.

Artie heard her tone and stopped all his faffing about. Artie looked from Dr Jennings to his daughter, and an uncomfortable silence settled over the little room.

"What?" Artie demanded. "What is wrong?"

Artie sat down, and Dr Jennings gently began to explain what had happened to Isla and the injuries that she had endured.

"She wasn't trampled by a horse then?" asked Artie.

"No, Sir," answered Dr Jennings.

Artie looked down at his hands and began to drum his fingers on the table. Suddenly he slammed his fist onto the wood then grabbed Simon Jennings by his collar.

"Why are you only telling me now?" Artie shouted at the doctor.

"Stop it, Pa, leave him alone. I didn't want you to know."

"By Jove, Isla!" Artie Dickson exploded, "how can you have kept this from me? What in God's name were you thinking of, since when have we ever had secrets from each other."

"It happened to me, not you," shouted Isla.

"Of course, it happened to me. You are my daughter. You are my everything."

Artie was furious, and for Isla, the room was becoming smaller and smaller. She couldn't breathe. She ran to the front door and swung it open. She stood on the top step and scooped in deep breaths, trying to calm down.

"Artie, there is more. Isla is pregnant."

"And how long have you known this, Simon?" Artie shouted at the doctor.

"I only diagnosed it yesterday, Artie. That is why I am here. I wanted to tell you myself."

"Who did this? Has anyone been arrested yet? Isla, who did this to you?"

"I don't know Pa, it was dark, and he was covered, and then he hurt me so badly that I couldn't move," Isla said it all matter of fact, all her reserves of self-pity were depleted.

"Who is she protecting?" Artie snarled at the young doctor.

"That is a terrible accusation, Artie. The situation is terrible as it is. Isla will gain nothing by you losing your mind."

Artie wanted to beat someone or something. He wanted to destroy everything he saw. He took his hat and charged out of the tiny one-roomed apartment and into the street. Artie headed for the dirtiest pub on the bad side of St Ives. He shoved his way to the bar, elbowing rough types out of his way as he barged forward. Artie was aggressive, and it wasn't long before a bar fight ensued. It was an epic battle, so much so that his boss had to bail him out of gaol and Artie's name was in the newspaper headlines the following morning.

16

TOBY JOE

Isla was too young to withstand the shame of her condition amongst the people of St Ives. They had watched her grow from a girl to a woman, and now she was a fallen one. She would never reveal how the child was conceived. That would have been even more of a disgrace. Isla couldn't stand the little room she and her father lived in, and she couldn't bear her father's false bravado and forced cheer.

"I can't stay here anymore, Pa."

"What do you mean, lass?"

"I can't make a life here, Pa," she persisted.

"But this is your home. I will look after you. There is nothing to be ashamed of," Artie tried to console her.

"No, Pa, we both know that I will be the talk of the town."

"At least it will be people you know doing the talking."

"No, Pa. I want to be alone, anonymous."

"Where will you go?" Artie asked.

"Falmouth"

"What will you do there?"

"I will work in a market or scrub floors."

"You will have a bairn in yer tummy lass," Artie mumbled.

"I will not be the only woman working with a child in my stomach," she spat out.

Artie could feel her resentment, and he felt the same. His daughter was being cheated out of a normal life. Her child would always carry a stigma unless Isla spun a web of lies, which he would encourage her to do.

*

Artie gave Isla all his savings.

"I can't take this Pa, it's all that you have."

"Take it," he forced the money into her hand, "if I didn't lose everything, you would never have been in this mess. I am responsible for everything that has happened to you."

"Stop it, Pa, I don't want to ever hear you say that again. It is just a new start. Perhaps a new start will make me feel better."

Artie watched Isla leave. She left by train, and Artie broke down on the platform while he watched the train chug down the rails. Artie could never have predicted this day, all because a coward of a man beat and raped his beautiful child, destroying her body, mind, and future.

Artie Dickson was an Anglican and had always been, but today he was desperate to speak to somebody. He didn't have time to wait for an appointment with the local minister, so he made his way to the Catholic Church. He stood at the entrance and looked in. All the years of being warned away from the Roman church, he was surprised to see how similar it was to the church he attended there than the statues of the Holy Mother and the confession boxes.

He could smell smoke from the burning candles mingled with sweet incense. Oak benches, so heavy that ten men needed to lift one, had been lovingly preserved with oil and dusters. The warm yellow glow of candles flickered off the brass candelabra. The atmosphere was gentle, and for the first time in months, he felt at peace.

He wasn't sure of the procedure, so he knocked on the door to the confession box.

"Just come in," a voice instructed him.

Artie opened the door and collapsed onto the bench with all his weight and sorrow.

"You are new," said a mature Irish voice.

"Yes."

"Reverend Grainger will not be happy that you are here."

"Then don't tell him you saw me," chuckled Artie.

"How can I help you, Artie?"

"You know who I am?"

"Of course, I do," I would recognise that chuckle anywhere, the Priest said in good humour.

"Father, forgive me for I have sinned, and I have never made a confession. Perhaps this is God's way of punishing me."

"What have you done, Artie?"

There was a pause.

"Nothing, Father, absolutely nothing. There is a man I want to kill, but I do not know who or where he is. I lay in my bed and curse him; I curse him to death."

"What has he done to you, Artie?" asked the voice behind the screen.

"He has killed my daughter."

"As in murdered her?"

"No," replied Artie, slowly telling the priest everything he knew.

*

Father O' Grady leaned against the screen and listened to Artie's story. He had heard similar cases so many times before, and it never failed to sicken him. He could empathise with Artie Dickson. He had a mother and sisters in the old country, and he too would have protected them with his life and taken his chances with hellfire and brimstone.

"Where is she now?" asked Father O'Grady.

"She has left St Ives and gone to live in Falmouth."

"Do you have family there?"

"No, Father, she is alone."

"The Sisters of St Bernadette have a convent in Falmouth. I will write them a letter, but Falmouth is large, and it will be like finding a needle in a haystack."

"Would you really do that for me? I am not a Catholic."

"I know, but you are a human, and God doesn't discriminate."

Artie smiled to himself.

"Will she ever be my old Isla again?" Artie asked, a lump in his throat.

"You have raised the girl since she was twelve. You know her spirit. Today she may be broken, but be patient. If her spirit is as beautiful as you tell me, it will resurrect itself. Isla the Child will never come back, but Isla the Woman will be majestic.

*

Isla paid two weeks rent in advance for a room above a tavern situated on the wharf. Toby Joe's stood on the shady side of the harbour, and at night it was home to rough types. The window looked out on a back alley, and the smell from the rubbish was so strong that she couldn't open the window for fear of being ill. Being three months pregnant added insult to injury. There were many mornings when she heaved all her breakfast into a bucket.

The walls were damp with mould, and a small bed with a rickety headboard was pushed up against a wall. Besides that, there was a chair, a washstand and a cupboard. Everything was damaged, and people had carved their names out on the cupboard. It didn't help that the names could evoke fear in a reasonable man or woman's mind. John Dagger Brownlee had carved a dagger piercing a heart with blood running down the side. Gather Le Clerq used his artistic eye to draw a woman impaled on a stake.

Isla had not seen the gruesome images when she accepted the room on the dark winter night. She was just desperate for a bed. Blue paint peeled off the door and revealed green paint underneath. Where the green paint peeled, it was white. The white paint told Isla that long ago, someone had hope for the place.

*

Nights above the Toby Joe were long and rowdy. Music floated up from the tavern below. The ditties were contemporary and recognisable, but only just. The narrow-cobbled streets that led off the wharf reminded Isla of scenes out of Treasure Island. The only quiet night was

Sunday, and the pub became eerie in its silence. It was the jaunt of every 'ne'er do gooders' in Falmouth. A few women lived in rooms on the same floor as Isla, and it took a week to realise that they were working girls. Oddly, they had hearts of gold and embraced her as part of the large dysfunctional family whose lives revolved around 'The Joe'.

Sherry Brandy, not her real name, was the epicentre of all activity at The Joe. As she told Isla:

"When you've been and seen what I have, lass,
you don't want to remember who you are in the
morning," she put her head back and gave a loud
bellow, which got everyone in stitches.

Sherry's words resonated with Isla. Although young and naïve, all Isla longed for was that she would miscarry the child in her belly. She would save enough money to buy a passage on the first mail ship that stopped in Falmouth.

"How far along are you then?" Sherry asked Isla
one morning.

Isla wanted to cringe with embarrassment.

"Come now, young Isla, you have been sick every
morning this week. We have all heard you."

"Mind your own business, Sherry, leave me
alone."

Sherry looked at her with sincere empathy written all over her face.

"I know how you feel, lass, trust me. If anybody knows how you feel, it's Sherry Brandy."

*

After a week, Isla still didn't have a job. One morning, on her way down the stairs, Isla caught Sherry coming up.

"Where are you off to then?" Sherry called out to her.

"I'm going to the fish factory to look for a job."

"Joey wants to know if you can wash bottles and glasses."

"Of course, I can."

"Good, then be downstairs at four o'clock this afternoon. There is a job for you."

Isla couldn't believe her luck. It was as if a huge weight was lifted from her shoulders.

*

Sherry rushed downstairs and pushed "The Joe's" door open, and went inside with the force of a tornado. Joe looked up at her. He was familiar with Sherry's theatrics, but she was the heart and soul of the place, and he endured her for the sake of peace and profit.

"Is the wind howling out there?" Joe asked.

"Not at all," Sherry answered boldly.

"You've come off the street like a hurricane is chasing you."

"You have just hired a bottlewasher," Sherry announced.

Joey straightened up from behind the bar counter where he was backing bottles of 'not so legal' whiskey. He looked at her and shook his head.

"I already have two."

"I've already given her the job. I told her you agreed. You can't go back on your word now."

Joey was annoyed. Sherry kept on bloody doing this. She brought every stray back to 'The Joe," whether it was a cat, dog, or human.

"Alright," agreed Joey.

Sherry smiled in delight. She had known that Joey would agree.

"I'm paying the new girl out of your wages. I think that's fair and all."

"What?" Sherry was confused.

"Stop bringing new people into this establishment, Sherry. I know that you have a heart of gold, but we've almost got more workers than customers."

"She's in a terrible way Joey, she's young and really knows nothing of the streets. She must come from a good house 'cos she speaks posh."

Sherry left out the part about Isla's pregnancy.

"Please, Joey, I'm begging you, I'll give you all the favours you ask for."

"You owe me so many favours, Sherry. You may as well move into my house."

It was true. Sherry didn't know if she would have enough nights to repay him for what he had done for her.

"Get her in here by four. Show her the ropes. And keep her out of my way. I might sack her if I see her."

Sherry knew that Joey was all talk, but she had taken a wild chance. Thankfully it paid off.

18

THE SMUGGLER

At precisely four o'clock, Isla stepped into 'The Joe.' She stood inside the door and looked around her. She had never been inside a Tavern before, and acknowledged that she had not missed anything by staying out of them. The regulars were having a good stare at her, which made her feel self-conscious and exposed. It felt as if every man in the room knew what was under her dress. The thought made her panic. Any one of these men could have been her assailant. Isla was sure that everyone was looking at her midriff knowingly. There was nothing to show yet, but Isla still pulled her stomach in.

Sherry appeared from nowhere. She was all smiles.

"I can't work here, Sherry. I can't work with all these men."

"Just follow me to the back sweetheart, we will keep you far away from all these old bar flies."

Isla followed Sherry nervously.

"Use the back door if it makes you feel better, lass, it's always open."

Isla nodded.

The area where Isla would work was a shambles. There were two other young women there, and Sherry introduced them with a flourish.

"Sybil, Michelle, this is Isla. She is here to help lighten your load."

Sybil and Michelle burst out laughing.

Isla looked from Sherry to Sybil and then at Michelle.

"Oh love," laughed Michelle, taking Isla's hand. "There are so many people working back here. There is hardly much to do."

Isla gave a little smile and looked around her.

"Sherry feels sorry for everybody," smiled Sybil. "She collects people."

"Come now," said Michelle, "crack a smile. You are safe here. Let me show you around."

*

Isla wrote to Artie and told him that she had found a job, made friends, and worked for a kind man who ran an eating establishment. Most of it was true, and Joey did serve the occasional pasties over the counter. She didn't feel it necessary to tell him more, so she told him about the town, chatted about the weather, and went to great lengths to convince him that her lodgings were clean and comfortable. She signed the letter with a flourish and PS'd that she loved him very much.

It was Sunday afternoon, and Isla made her way to the High Street. She put the letter into the post box, then made her way down to the waterfront. Isla stood at the water's edge, watching the gulls and the small fishing boats in the harbour. She looked across the Carrick Roads and was temporarily mesmerized by the flashing lamp of the lighthouse.

It was becoming cold, and the light was fading. The strollers had vanished, and Isla realised that she was by herself. She saw a man in the distance. He looked in a hurry as he scurried along.

Isla suddenly felt fear. She wanted to get away. She turned around and began to walk towards 'The Joe." She looked over her shoulder. The man was getting closer. Now she was consumed by full-blown panic. She began to run but kept looking back, like a terrified deer trying to outrun the hunter. Isla was so afraid that she wasn't watching her step, her skirt swished around her legs, and she stood on the hem of her skirt. She went flying forward. She put out her hands to break the fall and landed on them, grazing them on the rough cobbled path. She was on her hands and knees, and his footsteps stopped behind her.

"Let me help you up," said a firm voice.

Isla put her hand out to stop him.

"I can get up by myself," she insisted, "don't touch me."

The stranger didn't say anything as he looked at her motionless.

"Are you well enough to go further by yourself?"
he asked

"Of course," she snapped, brushing her skirt off
and lifting her chin up in an attempt to disguise
her embarrassment.

He looked down at her and smiled. She noticed he had close-clipped light brown hair, and the gold highlights in between caught the last light of the afternoon. He had about two days' worth of beard, which was scruffy yet attractive. His skin was tanned from the elements, and his blue eyes were compassionate and alert.

He took a few steps back, still observing her closely.

"You seem to be alright. Do you mind if I leave
you here? I have to get going. The sun is fading"

Without waiting for thanks or a greeting, Brae Prideaux hopped over the low stone wall and landed on the sand below. Isla watched him running towards a small boat, which would take him across the Carricks Road to the lighthouse, where she presumed he lived.

*

'The Joe' opened early on a Monday morning. Whether rain or shine, the regulars sat on the wall, overlooking the harbour, impatient for the sign to read 'open'.

Joey's most profitable day of the week was a Monday when his clientele drank enough to make up for Sunday.

The Monday crowd was never rowdy. They were humble, grateful and desperate to sink some grog into their thirsty bodies. Isla was working an early shift, and she noticed two newcomers whom she had never seen in the tavern before.

"Sherry has taken herself off to her ma this morning. I believe that the old dame is sick. I need some help behind the bar for a few hours. We're busier than normal."

"Of course, Joe, I'll get cracking."

Joey had watched Isla for some time. Isla had worked at his alehouse for a month. At first, she had been shy, too afraid to say boo to a goose, but she had started to thaw, and underneath the shield was a kind, sweet girl. She was a looker as well, and he bet to himself that she had a story to tell.

*

Ashwin Jones thumped his large fist on the bar counter. The Welshman was the size of a Titan, and Joey had never seen him before.

"Fecking spring tide, can't stand it. Slows everything down. Give me another jar, will you? I've got a one hell of a thirst on me this morning."

Isla fetched him a pint of ale and set it down on the counter in front of him. Ashwin Jones took one look and swept it off the table with the back of his hand. It landed with an ear-splitting crash.

"Rum," he commanded.

Isla showed no reaction. She found a bottle of rum from the smuggled stock and put it in front of him.

"You are a pretty little thing, you are."

Isla recognised the man as aggressive, and she didn't like him. She also knew that if she didn't pacify him, he had the nature to become worse.

"Thank you, Sir," she replied coyly.

"S'pose, every man in Falmouth is after a little maiden like you," growled Jones.

"No, Sir."

Ashwin Jones had used many women, but in his circles, there was never someone as fair as this.

"Are you a virgin?" he shouted for all the tavern to hear, then doubled over and laughed.

Everybody in the tavern thought it was funny as well. The legless, toothless and hopeless all joined in to have a good old belly laugh at her expense. Isla blushed and tried to block out the humiliating jeers.

They were still having a good old chortle when the front door opened. Isla recognised the man who had tried to help her the evening before.

Brae Prideaux was in a hurry and walked over to Joey without acknowledging anyone around him.

"Morning, Joey," the visitor greeted.

"You're in early today."

"Collecting the post, then back to the heads."

"Who's out there with you?"

"Old Paddy Livingstone from up the coast, trustworthy bloke, wouldn't have it any other way."

"Good lad. What do you need? I only see you when you want something."

Brae Prideaux's laugh had a sincere ring to it.

"The bloke who wanted to buy my boat. Tell him it's for sale if he comes in here again."

"Right then. You buying a new one?"

"Yep, found a bucket in Derry, steam, so she is, strong as Russia."

The laughter and cajoling in the tavern were deafening, and both men turned around to see what had caused such mirth.

"Well, there you are then, lads, the lady is a virgin. I think I must marry her. Virgins are hard to find where I come from."

Isla's eyes watered, and Joey watched the tears of humiliation stream down her cheeks. She wiped them away with the back of her hand. He walked over to her.

"Go on to the back, Isla, I will take over from here."

"Not the usual kind who lives upstairs now, is she?" guffawed Ashwin, which resulted in another round of bone grinding cruelty.

Ashwin was enjoying himself now, and he was playing to the gallery.

"Another drink?" Joey asked.

"Bring the girl back out here Joey, she is easy on the eye."

Joey sensed that the mood in the tavern was turning, and he didn't want the tavern broken down on the most profitable day of the week. He turned away and saw Brae Prideaux at the bar counter. Brae was a tough one. He had grown up working on his father's fishing boats until he went to the University of London. Five years later, he returned to St Mawes with an engineering degree and was immediately awarded the position of lighthouse keeper. Although he was an educated man, he was also a native of Cornwall, and he wouldn't allow a coarse Welshman to intimidate him.

Brae walked up to Ashwin and slapped him hard on the back.

"What d'you think you're up to, mate?"

"Come on, old man," smiled Brae good-naturedly, "you've got a bit of tide to take you up the Carricks. If you don't leave now, you will still be here tomorrow."

"Ta for the heads-up, Brae, I've not been watching the time, only the girl."

Joey breathed a sigh of relief and silently gave thanks that Brae Prideaux had a head on him.

Brae watched Ashwin swagger down to the harbour, he didn't like the man, and he never had. Everyone knew that under the auspices of running a legitimate business Ashwin smuggled every commodity that he could lay his hands on. He was cunning and ingenious because the authorities always found the goods but could never trace them back to Ashwin Jones and his fleet of boats.

*

Monday morning, one week later, Ashwin Jones was back at 'The Joe." This time he tried to behave himself.

"I can't get the girl out of my mind," he lamented to Joey.

"Come now, Ashwin, she is way too young for a man like you. You want a woman with a little experience."

"I want a new experience, Joey. I like the idea of an innocent young thing catering to my every need."

Joey shook his head.

> "Call her in, let me take her to tea up the road
> there. Maybe I can talk some sense into her,"
> Ashwin winked at him.

At that moment, Isla arrived at the tavern. When she saw Ashwin Jones, she turned and left. It was Ashwin's golden opportunity to follow her and introduce a milder version of himself. Ashwin stood up, paid his bill, and left the tavern. He saw Isla in the distance and hastened his pace to catch up with her.

> "Stop," he commanded.

Isla pretended not to hear him. She was terrified. As long as she was amongst people, she was safe. She knew a little tearoom a way on, and she was sure that he wouldn't dare follow her into it. She only relaxed when she heard the shop door slam behind her. She took her place at a table and ordered a cup of tea. As she waited, she heard the doorbell tinkle to announce another customer. She looked up. It was Ashwin Jones.

He looked out of place, making his way through the delicate tables and chairs towards her, the proverbial bull in a china shop. She was sitting in the darkest corner of the tearoom, a stupid attempt at being invisible. Ashwin sat down opposite her, and the chair creaked under his weight.

Isla didn't lift her eyes off the tablecloth.

> "I am looking for a woman. You will get my
> name," he continued matter of fact, confident that

the words were sufficient motivation for Isla to endear herself to him.

"My house is across from St Mawes, north St Anthony's. Nobody comes there except my workers. I will put a roof over your head and food in your belly. In return, you will observe my rules and serve my every need. You will have to know your place. It is my house. Nobody tells me what to do. If you behave yourself, I will marry you."

Isla lifted her eyes. Ashwin Jones was an unpleasant looking man. His wavy black hair was streaked with grey, which gave away his age, and the grey extended into his beard. He had a short fringe cut close to his hairline, and he combed it forward. It contrasted with his bright red, sweaty forehead. His nose was small, insignificant and asymmetrical, and while his middle teeth were perfect, the incisors forced themselves forward, making him look like a vampire pug. He was strong, but his hands were small and permanently balled into fists. He couldn't speak other than in a scoffing tone, but it was his eyes that spoke of his character. They were small, black and as hard as onyx, and the only time they smiled was when he was being cruel.

Isla nodded.

He stood up, pushed the chair back, dug in his pocket for some money, and threw it on the table.

"Hurry up," he told her abruptly.

*

Sherry looked at her in dismay.

"Jesus, Joseph, and Mary, Isla, what was going through your mind?"

"I have no choice, Sherry. The child needs a father," she pointed to her stomach, "perhaps there is a chance he will marry me and make me decent."

"Go fetch the man who got you in this way and make him marry you."

"I don't know who the father is, Sherry," Isla said matter of fact.

Isla felt so defeated that she didn't have the energy to become emotional when she told Sherry her story.

"Oh lass, I am so sorry."

"Not your fault Sherry."

"We will look after you. We are your family. Stay here. Ashwin will use you and ruin you, then toss you to the wolves."

"You know the child will never have a normal life. This way, it has a chance."

"Ashwin Jones is one of the vilest men in Cornwall, lass. You will never experience normal with him, Isla. You won't be the first woman up there. He's had others, they never stay long, and we never see or hear of them again."

"I will visit."

Sherry laughed wryly, "No, you won't, lass, you will be trapped out there, but if there is ever trouble, try and get a letter to us, we will always help you."

Isla and Sherry hugged. She was going to miss Sherry. This flamboyant, boisterous, bright woman, who had experienced a lot of the bad that the world had to offer, had taken her under her wing and become one of the best friends that she would ever have.

"Thank you, Sherry, thank you."

*

"What in God's name is she thinking? How can you let her do this, Sherry? You of all the bloody people in the world know what a monster Ashwin Jones is."

Sherry sat at the bar counter and shook her head.

"What am I to do, Joey?"

"I wonder who the coward was who raped her?" Joey looked murderous. I'd like to find him and geld him."

Any other evening Sherry and Joey would have had a laugh at the remark, but tonight it wasn't funny.

18

HELL'S COVE

Ashwin Jones had no real intention of marrying Isla - his words rang hollow. He had already had three wives, and they had just caused him trouble. This one was young and innocent. He could mould her to suit himself. With a little discipline, she would be ideal. If anyone asked why she was there, he would introduce her as a maid.

Isla stood on the cliffside and looked down on the small cove below. They had to drive the cart through small woods to reach the road that led down to the small bay. She tried to ignore the trees around her. The long shadows were ominous and gave her a gloomy premonition of what lay ahead.

Halfway down the hill, they were met by an interesting man sufficiently so as to take Isla's mind off her surroundings.

"Good evening, Master," he bellowed at them.

"Get ahead and open the gates," Ashwin yelled at him.

"Sid," growled Ashwin, "stay away from him."

Isla had the impression that Sid was a simpleton, and it was another bad omen.

Sid ran ahead and reached a gate that he opened, joyfully humble. Ashwin drove through, clearly Lord of his Manor.

"Shut," he commanded Sid.

People appeared from everywhere, mostly men, and gathered around the cart as if their Master had arrived to bring the good news. Ashwin stood upon the cart, and the men stared up at him with reverence.

"Stand up," he ordered Isla.

She complied, uncertain of his intentions.

"Nobody touches her. She is mine," roared the mighty Ashwin Jones.

A hush fell over the men. Only one man had ever dared touch Ashwin's woman, and he had been tied to the rocks and battered by the elements until he died, dried and burnt from sun and salt.

"Prepare the boats, two long and one steamer. Twenty-four men, two coxswains. We sail at midnight."

Ashwin breathed fear into the compound, and it became a bustling hub of activity. Driven by her future husband's cruelty and motivated by fear, Isla stood next to him, feeling exposed. The eyes of every man were on her.

"Take her to the house," Ashwin instructed Sid.

Sid helped her from the cart, and he walked ahead of her, hopping over and stepping around debris that littered the yard. The place had an eerie, mediaeval feel about it, and Isla wished that she had never agreed to marry Ashwin Jones.

*

Sid showed her into the kitchen. It was neat and clean, albeit old.

"What must I do?" Isla asked him.

"I do everything for you and the master," giggled Sid.

Isla studied him. He was skinny with sandy blonde hair, and had two buck teeth. He had an airy but kind look about him, as if nothing much phased him.

The house stood against the cliff. It was built out of rocks and had a thatch roof. The long low house blended into its surroundings and was perfectly camouflaged against the rock face. It overlooked a small cove with deep waters, a perfect natural harbour. It was cluttered with boats of all types: long boats, small rowing boats, two sailboats, and a small steamer.

Sid showed her into the room that she would share with Ashwin Jones. On one side was a door that led outside.

"Steps to privy," Sid giggled and pointed to the door.

"Lovely cupboard," Sid pointed and smiled proudly and pointed to a rickety box that would suffice as a cupboard.

Although it was warm, there was nothing sophisticated about the place. The damp sea reached everything with its salty claws, and there were patches of black mould on the walls. In the middle of the room was a large bed covered by animal and sheep skins.

Isla felt transported back to a dark age, a place of gloom and miserable cruelty.

*

Sid closed the heavy wooden door and left Isla alone. Ashwin had brought several women back to his room, but they never stayed very long. Sid would just wake up in the morning, go off to the house to do his job and find the woman missing.

Isla was the prettiest woman that Ashwin had ever brought home. In fact, she was beautiful, and Sid wondered how Ashwin had convinced her to leave her life behind and follow him into the bellows of hell. He felt sorry for Isla. She was still very young, likely with little experience, which was the very thing that Ashwin's sick mind desired. He would dominate and defile her, then hand her to the other men to enjoy what was left. Suddenly, out of the blue, she would disappear, and when Sid asked where the miss was, he always got the same answer, 'none of your business, fool.'

For years Sid had acted the fool. It was what saved him from Ashwin Jones' murderous wrath. Ashwin was confident that Sid was mental, which meant that Sid got away with seeing and hearing a lot more than anyone else did. And as long as Sid was bouncing about like the village idiot, Ashwin became more and more complacent, going as far as to appoint Sid a houseboy.

But Sid wasn't daft, nor a village idiot or the court fool. He had been employed by Ashwin Jones when he was fifteen and very soon learnt what it would take to survive in the presence of evil. Within the first week of observing life in Hell's Cove, as it was called by the men, he decided that he didn't want to be a smuggler. Firstly, the operation was run by brutish men who had no respect for life or the law and secondly, he didn't want to go to gaol. It would break his mother's heart. He needed the money because his parents were struggling tenant farmers, and work was scarce. Sid couldn't leave. Besides, Ashwin Jones would give him a good flogging to prove what was in for him should he ever shoot his mouth off.

The only option he had was to behave like a simpleton. To convince Ashwin Jones of this was a doddle. Sid pursued a course of over ingratiating himself to his master. He smiled and indulged his master's most unreasonable demands, but when he was sent to work with the other men, he was as clumsy and unintelligent as he could act.

The men complained about Sid, yet Ashwin was comfortable with the idiot that flitted around him. He was a harmless fool who lacked any intelligence to decipher the complex web of evil that Ashwin wove. Sid was agreeable, ingratiating, humble, showed the delight of a child when praised, ridiculed or punished: In truth, Sid was brilliant, the only idiot in Hell's Cove who would walk away innocent of criminal activity. The act had taken mental agility and months of absolute focus, but he had achieved his goal.

Sid's ma didn't have long to live, and the brilliant village idiot had devised an ingenious plan which would free him from Hell's Cove and buy him a ticket to the other end of the world.

*

Ashwin got into the kitchen, threw his hat onto the table and looked at Sid.

"I'm sailing at high tide. I'm collecting supplies in the channel. If I get cold, I'll whip the skin off your back."

Sid gave an exaggerated giggle.

"Are you a girl?" Ashwin scowled at him.

"No master, no," Sid continued to chuckle.

"Take the cover off the pit as well. We are getting six African visitors."

Sid nodded. His eyes were full of adoration for his master.

"Yes, yes, master, of course, master."

"I want the chains dragged from the barn and put in the pit even if it takes all night."

Sid wasn't paying enough attention to Ashwin's liking.

"I'll lock you up in there with them stupid slaves," bellowed Ashwin. His eyes were bulging, but Sid kept his wits about him, "get on with it, you bloody monkey."

Sid doubled up in mirth, giggling till the tears ran down his face.

Out of frustration, Ashwin picked up a clay jug and hurled it across the kitchen, and it crashed into a thousand pieces as it hit the wall behind Sid's head.

Sid made big eyes and exaggeratedly fled on tip toe out of the kitchen.

Ashwin longed to wallop Sid at times, but he suppressed the urge because, albeit it was tedious, Sid followed his every instruction to the letter. Sid never gossiped or connived. He seldom remembered facts and events and distanced himself from the other men.

Sid went towards the pit, a hole dug to hide contraband liquor. He opened the heavy iron lid and pulled the chains behind him. The large links made a soft, high-pitched sound as they fell against each other. It was the unmistakable sound of confinement, torture, slavery. It made any prisoner's heart pound with fear.

It had never crossed Sid's mind that the evil Welshman was smuggling slaves. If he was caught, he would face the gallows without prejudice.

*

Isla heard the jug explode in the kitchen, followed by heavy footsteps that became louder as they got closer to the bedroom door. She knew that it was Ashwin, and she tried to say something when he opened the door. Ashwin Jones' large body filled the doorway.

Isla stood on the opposite side of the bed to Ashwin. He looked down at Isla. She was by far the most beautiful woman he had ever chosen.

Ashwin fished in his pocket and pulled out a small leather pouch with a drawstring. He threw it across the bed, and it landed in front of her.

"Open it."

Isla undid the draw strings and opened the pouch. Inside was a silver ring with a purple stone. It was antique and ornate.

"It's lovely," she whispered.

"Put it on."

Isla slipped the ring onto her finger.

"Put it on your ring finger."

Isla inhaled sharply and complied.

"You are my wife."

Isla looked at him and frowned. She had expected a wedding, a church, a dress, a license, but this was what marriage meant to Ashwin Jones. It was his land, his cove, and his rules. She consoled herself that he had given her a ring and proclaimed them husband and wife, which was a sign of respect.

"Thank you," she gave a small smile.

She didn't know that there were many women who had been given the ring minutes before Ashwin Jones consummated their unorthodox marriage.

Isla watched the Welshman undress. His stomach was round from overeating, his belly button was popping, and he was covered in black hair. His toes were short and stubby, and his feet were small like his hands. All she could think of when she looked at him was the ugliest man that she had ever seen.

Ashwin walked over to her, and when he reached her, he pushed her onto the bed.

"Take off your clothes. I'm in a hurry."

Isla got undressed and closed her eyes. She was prepared for this eventuality, and she wouldn't fight. She would let him do it.

The Welshman's eyes studied her body hungrily and stopped at her belly. There was a swelling that was out of proportion to the rest of her torso. Ashwin grabbed her hair and pulled her face around to look at him. His eyes radiated cold, brutal cruelty, intent on hurting her as much as he could. Fury was etched upon his craggy features.

He pulled her towards him and spat at her cheek. Isla used the back of her hand to wipe off the warm stale spital running down her soft clean skin. Ashwin could see open terror on Isla's face.

"You've been used, you little sow, and I don't want a used-up nanny goat in my bed."

Ashwin ripped the ring off Isla's finger, and it scraped the top layer of skin off from knuckle to tip.

"Did you think that you could hide that bump from me? Did you think you could fool me into thinking your little runt was mine? Do you think I am a fool?"

"I am sorry, I was scared," she said, trying to explain her situation.

Ashwin had no empathy, and accused her of flaunting, taunting and seducing her rapist to the point that he had no control over his actions.

"That's a lie," she yelled at him.

"I will show you what happens when you call me a liar," his voice boomed through the house."

This time Isla couldn't feel sorry for herself. She had been stupid, stupid, stupid.

Ashwin balled his little hand into a fist and planted a solid blow against her temple. Isla's head jerked to the side, and saliva exploded out of her mouth. She tumbled to the stone floor, landing on her face. Isla's teeth cut through her lips, causing her mouth to be purple and bloody, instantly swelling to twice their size. Blood poured from the wound on her forehead, and it ran into her eyes.

Ashwin felt no shame or remorse. Isla was just a thing to use, and the thing had disappointed him. It was all her own fault. She should have known better. Nobody in Hell's Cove would cross him. It was all his.

*

Ashwin threw Isla down on the kitchen floor. She was still unconscious, and her head cracked on the floor, causing another wound and more blood.

Sid met his master as he made his way back to the house from the pit. Sid could see that the man was enraged and kept a safe distance from him, yet always acting the simpleton.

"The wench was in the bed of another man before she married me," said the Welshman between his teeth.

"You know what happens to women who make a fool out of me."

Sid nodded. Eyes were as wide as saucers.

"I'd give her to you to finish off if you weren't retarded. Probably wouldn't know where to put it."

Sid giggled.

"Give her to the men, let them have her when they've had enough, tell them to drown her."

*

Sid didn't move until he saw Ashwin reach the small jetty below and board the steamer. He only relaxed a little when the boat began to move, pulling the long boats next to it. As they sailed past the headland into the open sea, Sid turned around and sprinted to the house. He had anticipated that Isla would be in the bedroom. Instead, he found her on the kitchen floor.

Isla's face was a bloody mess. Sid sat her up against the wall. She was only half-conscious.

"Come on, girl, open your eyes for me," whispered Sid.

Isla slowly opened her eyes, she was confused, but she recognised Sid.

"Sid?" She groaned.

"Yes."

"I am going to take you away from here," Sid whispered. "You must trust me."

Sid got a bowl of water and cleaned her face. Her bodice was soaked with blood, but he had to get her out of "Hell's Cove" and be back by sunrise.

Sid wrapped a large oilskin around Isla and lifted her onto the mule. He climbed up and sat behind her, steadying her against his body. He pointed the mule into the forest, hoping that the stubborn animal would cooperate. It was the only animal on four legs strong and stupid enough to endure the treacherous climb. Sid coaxed the animal up a steep, narrow path, thick with treacherous shale, roots and hanging foliage. They reached the top of the cliff and exited the protective canopy of trees that had hidden them. There was no moon. The only beacon was the flashing lamp of the lighthouse.

*

Brae Prideaux, St Anthony's lighthouse master, sat in his study that overlooked the Carrick Roads and the sea to the south. He was at peace, semi-mesmerised by the flashing light as he followed it, using it as a torch to illuminate the churning water and watch for the occasional boat or ship passing the treacherous piece of coast.

Brae heard hooves approaching his cottage. It didn't sound as if the rider was in a hurry, and the animal was walking slowly. Brae opened the cottage door and stepped out into the crisp sea air. Nobody came up there at night, it was a good distance from St Mawes, and the ferry only ran in daylight hours. Brae saw the silhouette of the large mule, as it came closer, until it was fully illuminated by the oil lamps that lined the path to the lighthouse.

Brae saw Sid with a woman sitting in front of him, slumped to one side. The man had his arms around her waist, trying to keep her from falling and attempting to steer the mule at the same time. The lighthouse keeper stepped into the animal's path.

Sid didn't greet him. He had no time for niceties.

"Brae, I've got a problem here. You have to help me."

There was a new person in Sid's body, and Brae was confused, someone way brighter than the man he occasionally met at Ashwin's side.

"Sid?"

"Help me, get her down," Sid told Brae, who rushed forward and caught Isla as she slipped out of the saddle.

Brae looked at the girl's face, shocked by her wounds.

"Ashwin will surely kill her if she stays at Hell's Cove."

Brae stared at Sid, bewildered.

"Please get a message to Falmouth. The navy must close in on the cove after sunrise."

Brae frowned in confusion.

"I've been a spy in Hell's Cove for four years. We've waited for the day that Jones makes a mistake, and he has. He's bringing in slaves. If I don't live to see the day, he will hide them in a pit under the pig pen."

Brae shuddered at the thought of trading in lives.

"This time, he will hang, and all his men with him."

"Go on, Sid, I'll get the message out. Don't worry about the girl. I'll get her better."

Brae Prideaux hurried into the cottage and lay Isla on the sofa. It was imperative he send the message.

The admiral of the British Navy was awoken in the early hours of the morning with an urgent telegram.

The despicable Welsh slave trader Ashwin Jones had sealed his own fate. The admiral's orders were to capture Jones and his men alive and scuttle their small fleet.

19

THE LIGHTHOUSE

Brae helped Isla to the bedroom and put her into bed. He looked at her face and shook his head.

"You are the girl from the waterfront. You were working at 'The Joey.'"

"Yes."

"Did Jones do this to you?"

"Yes," she sighed, exhausted, "I guess I deserved it."

"Mmm. You are more stupid than I already think you are."

Isla's eyes fluttered, and she glared at him.

'Good," Brae thought to himself, 'she still has some spirit left in her."

"What earned you this thrashing that you so deserved?" he asked her sarcastically.

"He was going to marry me, then found out that I was pregnant by another man."

Brae laughed softly.

"Forgive me for being callous, but you are not the first person to receive that promise and be put out the same night."

"He had good reason to," Isla claimed responsibly.

"It's the second time you say so. Perhaps if you say it a third time, I'll believe you," he retaliated. "Your only fault was believing what he told you."

"He lay down the rules. I knew what he was. The child needs a name, and it was the only opportunity I had to give it one."

"It?"

"The child isn't mine. I didn't choose to conceive it, and I don't want it."

Brae was taken aback by straightforward answers, but Isla was far beyond pride. It was what it was, and no amount of shame would change that.

"What time does the ferry leave tomorrow?"

"It arrives at midday and leaves at three o'clock."

"I'll go back to 'The Joe,' at least I'll have work," Isla said firmly

"When is the baby coming?"

"Three months," she looked away in shame.

"You look terrible. You can't work at 'The Joe' looking like a purple pincushion. Even the scum who go there have an expectation of what a pretty face should be."

"I have no choice," Isla countered.

"Oh, stop that rot," Brae roared. "We all have choices. Yours have been poor."

"Don't be judgemental," said Isla as she stood up and slowly walked towards the door.

"Do you have money for the ferry and a coat to cover that blood-stained dress?"

Isla looked down at her bodice. It was a mess.

"Yes, I have a coat. I have no money.

"You can always do me a favour, and I will pay for the ferry," he smiled at her.

Isla lifted her hand in a flash and slapped him so hard that she left a hand mark across his cheek. He was surprised at her strength, given her condition.

"Don't ever speak to me that way again. Ashwin Jones was the last man who will ever abuse me."

Although Brae Prideaux was humiliated, she had also gained his respect. The young woman was far stronger than she appeared.

Isla limped to the cottage door, opened it, and walked into the dark. Brae followed her out.

"It's steep. You won't make it down there in the dark."

She ignored him flatly.

"You will sit out there all day without food or water."

Brae caught up with her and grabbed her by the arm. Isla swung around and slapped him for a second time. She also kicked him on the shin. Brae had to work hard not to show pain.

"I told you not to touch me."

"Alright, I am sorry," he put his hands up in the air in surrender, "I won't touch you again."

"Come back to the cottage, have something to eat, and I will make us a pot of tea. That dress needs a wash, and I think a good sleep will do you well."

Brae was ashamed of how he had treated her. She was right, he didn't know her story, and he had treated her harshly on the very night that another man had beaten her. What had he been thinking? He put out his hand to help her climb the path.

This time she allowed him to take it.

"I am sorry," he said.

"You should be."

*

Brae cared for Isla, doing everything he could to make up for his bad manners. On the second night, Isla cooked dinner of fish and potato, and they sat talking away into the night. Brae was surprised at Isla's education but was sceptical when he heard about Freya. Isla was reluctant to discuss her mother, and it was the first time in many years that she had given her any thought.

"Is she a good person?" Brae asked her.

"No, Brae, she is a very bad person. I have no desire to see her."

Brae was silent, lost in thought.

"What did she do to you?"

"She was cruel. She never cared for my father and me. Thank goodness that he was a good man and looked after me well. Who knows what would have happened otherwise?"

Brae wondered if she was paying attention to what she said. Surely, she could draw comparisons and appreciate that her child would suffer a worse fate than her mother if she was left at an orphanage.

"I guess you judge me by my mother's sins."

"I don't know," he shrugged, "I don't know who you are."

*

For the first time in almost seven months, Isla began to feel human. Since the night that she had left Victoria Manor, she had faced one shock after the next. Her stupid, desperate decision to marry Ashwin Jones had almost killed her, and it was a miracle that she had found herself in this peaceful place.

She faced every day in fear that she would have to leave and return to 'The Joe'. Granted, Sherry and Joey would accept her with open arms, but now that she was feeling better and thinking clearly, she couldn't envision a life living in the back alleys of Falmouth and working as a barmaid for the rest of her life.

Three days turned into four and then five. One morning Brae informed her that he had a job for her.

> "I need a maid to clean the cottage and the lighthouse. I can give you a small stipend. It will help you reach the mainland."

Isla grabbed the opportunity and set about keeping herself busy. Her personality slowly began to emerge as the hard shell she built around her began to crack. She also suffered days when a darkness descended upon her. She would relive the last six months, and look at her big stomach with resentment. The child had ruined everything. Every plan, desire and dream had departed the day that Dr Simon Jennings told her that she was to have a baby.

*

Brae and Isla sat in front of the fireplace. It was a cold night, and Isla sat under a blanket on the sofa. Brae had become fond of her. The more time he spent with her, the more attracted he was to her. She looked serene and beautiful in the warm glow of the fire. Her hair was long and fell around her face in waves, her eyes sparkled, and Brae caught himself staring at her.

Brae went across the room and sat next to her. He wasn't looking forward to saying goodbye. They laughed a lot, and she challenged him mentally. She had a gentle, lovely personality, and she found good and joy in everything.

"You are lovely," he murmured.

His eyes were soft, and his handsome face was close to Isla's.

She laughed softly. He had once been so fierce with her, and she with him, but now they sat next to each other like old friends.

"Can I touch you?" He asked softly, hopefully.

Her forehead wrinkled into a frown.

"The last time I did, you beat me up," he teased.

"Yes," she whispered.

He lifted his hand and touched her face gently. Then, he leaned forward and kissed her softly on her mouth. Isla didn't close her eyes but watched him as he kissed her, terrified that his closeness would develop into a violent interaction. She had never kissed a man romantically.

"Don't be afraid. I will never hurt you."

He moved away. He saw her stomach move under her dress. She was far along, and the baby wriggled.

Brae put his hand on Isla's stomach and felt the kick, kick, kick of the tiny feet just under her breasts. It enthralled him. He had never experienced it before, and the idea of a real life inside this beautiful woman was a miracle.

Isla pushed his hand away.

"I am sorry," he felt as if he had intruded on her privacy, but it was such a lovely moment.

"I've made inquiries," he said gently, afraid of upsetting her.

"There is a convent in Falmouth. There are midwives. You will be safe there. The baby will be safe."

He gently stroked her hair.

Brae could see the light fade from Isla's eyes and the moment between them.

"Sweetheart," he said gently, "you have to trust me. You and the baby have to be kept safe."

"I don't care about it," Isla snapped at him, "it's a monster. Anything that comes from the seed from a man so evil can only be a monster."

"And you, Isla? Are you a monster because your mother is a bad woman? Must I love you less because of your seed?" He stopped. He had shared his feelings for her at the wrong time. He had wanted to tell her when she could absorb and accept it.

"I don't even know who its father is," Isla hissed.

"Who do you believe it is, Isla, you must have a theory. Who would have done such a terrible thing to you?"

Isla felt resentful, and she spat out the story of her experience at the hands of her attacker.

"There must be something that you noticed about the man, something familiar. Anything, even the most insignificant detail."

"I have done my best to blot it out, else the thoughts would have turned into demons that stalked my every waking moment. I don't want to talk about it ever again, and I want to forget, every detail was a nightmare."

"Listen to me, Isla, you have to face the fact that you will give birth to this baby, and you will need somebody to help you. I can't help you with this. You have to help yourself."

The words hit home.

"I will have it, but I will not keep it."

Brae shook his head.

"What if I marry you? We will give it a life."

"No. I never want to see it. They can take it away and give it to whomever they please. Perhaps a young couple who cannot conceive and would adopt it and love it as their own? What's wrong with that?"

Brae was angry and disappointed. He loved Isla, but he couldn't accept her cold-hearted rejection of the child.

*

Isla couldn't sleep. Brae had said he loved her, but she knew that there was a condition attached. He was a man of principle, he would love her and marry her, but she would have to take responsibility for the child.

She, in turn, would remember the brutal rape every time she looked at its face, and she would hate it. She already hated it.

She heard Brae's question, 'what can you remember, Isla? You must remember something.'

She had spent more time trying to forget. Now, he wanted her to remember.

Even if he loved her, even if she had feelings for him, he was asking too much.

*

Isla finally began to doze off. She was in the fuzzy twilight between wake and sleep. Otherworldly images began to dominate her consciousness as she wove her way towards the total oblivion of sleep. In the last seconds of no man's dreamland, she stood in the centre of a forest, it spun around her, and she felt dizzy. It felt as if the trees were suffocating her, then the branches turned to hands. She looked down at them. All she saw was a black birthmark on the inside of the person's wrist.

Isla sat bolt upright. She remembered the birthmark as clear as day. She climbed off the bed and knocked on Brae's door.

"Brae," she called gently.

He opened his eyes and saw her standing next to his bed.

"I've remembered something, Brae, the man who attacked me had a black birthmark on the inside of his wrist."

20

DEBRA X

Isla gave birth to a child in the late hours of a Sunday night. She didn't want to see it, name it or know its gender. The nuns were used to young mothers in trouble. Isla wasn't the only woman to discard her child that week.

The young nun looked at the little girl, and her heart went out to the child. She announced her arrival in the world with violent protest, waving her arms and kicking her legs because she had been expelled from the warmth of her mother's womb.

"She is fierce for such a tiny thing," laughed Sister Bernadette.

Isla could hear the conversation on the other side of the room, and she tried to block her ears.

"We should give her a name, a no-nonsense name like Helga or Christina," said Sister Bernadette.

"Those are terrible names, Sister. Let us call her Debra. Debra was fierce and just."

Everything became quiet, and Isla was glad that the child was still and the nuns had stopped their nattering. It all grated on her nerves. As she finally began to relax and escape scrutiny, she heard an exclamation from the other side of the room:

"Oh my, Sister Bernadette! Just look at this. How unusual is this?"

Sister Bernadette flew across the room, expecting the worst.

"What is it? What is wrong?"

"Look at this," said the nun, "little Debra has a birthmark on the inside of her wrist."

Both women giggled and cooed, and Isla was devastated. She had been right. The man did have a birthmark on his wrist, and so did the child.

The nuns would take care of Debra in the nursery until she was weened, and then she would be put into a Catholic orphanage unless someone chose to adopt her. When she was older, she would likely find her way into a workhouse until she was old enough to work in a factory. The future for the child was grim. The local parishioners were too poor to adopt or support another mouth. The child was surrendered to her fate.

Against the nuns' orders, Isla left the small infirmary two days later. She rested with Sherry for a week until she felt fit. Joey gave her money, and Isla bought a train ticket to St Ives. Isla was a complicated ball of emotions, but she felt free. At last, her body was her own. For nine months, an unwanted stranger had occupied her.

Isla stood on the platform at the small station in St Ives. The world had changed a lot in six months. In reality, it was Isla who had changed. She carried her small suitcase down the hill, past whitewashed row houses with thatched roofs, towards the sea way down at the bottom. When she reached the harbour, she turned left into a damp alley and then walked up a ramp to the one-roomed flat that her father lived in.

She knocked on the door loudly. She heard Artie's cheerful voice telling her to wait a moment, and she heard him fumble with the keys, and then the key turned. The door swung open, and a roar of delight emanated from Artie's chest. He stepped forward, took his daughter into his arms and wouldn't let her go until she insisted and wriggled out of his grip.

It was good to see her father. She had missed his cheerful, positive personality.

"You are looking well, lass, so much better than when you left here," Artie smiled broadly.

Isla felt tearful.

"Now, now, none of that. This is a celebration."

Isla smiled through the tears, and Artie put on the kettle.

"Now, lass, who is looking after my grandchild while you are here?" Artie asked excitedly.

"I left it at the convent in Falmouth, Pa, the nuns are taking care of it."

"It?"

"I left the child with them," she couldn't look her father in the eye.

"Are they looking after the child for a few days while you are here?" Artie asked her, frowning in confusion.

"No, Pa, it will stay there for good."

"It?" Artie persisted. "Is it a boy or a girl? Does it have a name?"

"I don't know," she lied.

No matter where she went, the scrutiny wouldn't end. Her father, doctor, matron, Sherry and Joey and eventually Brae had interrogated her about her past, present, future. For nine months, she was forced to explain and justify herself. Now she sat in front of her father, who loved her with all his heart, and she lied to him without shame. She would do anything to end the constant harassment.

"That child would have meant the world to me," he said softly.

"Well, it will mean a lot to someone else too," she said harshly.

"Go and fetch the child Isla, or I will."

Isla shook her head. "No Pa, she even has the same mark on her wrist as her father, the man who raped me. I refuse to live with him in my mind every time I look at it."

Artie became furious with Isla.

"It, it, it!" he shouted, making Isla jump in her seat. "By God, Isla! This is a person we are talking about, not an anonymous 'it'. This is my grandchild, and I do not care for your shame or embarrassment. I am going to fetch her and raise her - I hope that I can do a better job raising her than I did you."

Those last words stung Isla.

Artie lifted his hat and coat off the peg. He left the cottage, slamming the door so hard that it echoed up and down the empty lanes of St Ives.

*

Brae Prideaux banged loudly on the gnarly oak door of the great convent. The setting around the building was scenic and picturesque, set in the middle of a well-kept garden.

Sister Magdalene opened the door and studied him from top to toe before she said a word.

"Good morning," she was polite but not friendly.

"Good morning, Sister," said Brae Prideaux. "My daughter was born here within the last two weeks. I have come to fetch her."

Sister Magdalene studied him for a few more seconds. In her experience, men were not inclined to claim children who were not their own, neither those who were.

"Come inside. Follow me."

Brae followed her to an office, it had an ornate vaulted ceiling, but it was sparse with only a crucifix against the wall.

The Mother superior sat behind a large desk. She had the upright posture of an army general and the same commanding presence.

"You may sit down, Mr Prideaux."

"Thank you, Mother," he said cordially.

"I believe that your child has been born here and is being cared for here."

"Yes, Mother," answered Brae.

"What was the mother's name?"

"Isla Dickson."

"What is your name?"

"Brae Prideaux. I am the Lighthouse keeper from over the Carrick Roads."

"Ah, I see, a professional man."

Brae nodded.

"Mr Prideaux, in my experience, men like you seldom discard their children or wives. Why not tell me the truth? Perhaps that will impress me more than the pretence that you are the child's father."

"Mother, before you go further, is it a boy or a girl?" asked Brae respectfully.

"It is a little girl. For now, we have named her Debra X."

Brae laughed loudly. It was a delightful sound and rang through the convent.

"Now tell me your story, Mr Prideaux. Debra X needs a good home, and I must decide whether you qualify for the job."

The Mother superior was satisfied and a little impressed with Brae's story. After all of the troubled new mothers they had seen at the convent, it was refreshing to see a decent man willing to take the responsibility of a child that was not his own.

The nuns nattered away while they led him to the nursery to meet the little girl that he had adopted. Sister Bernadette stood back and studied Brae's face as she put the baby in his arms.

He looked down at the little girl, awed that he had felt the little creature kicking in Isla's tummy only days ago. He could have sworn that she was the spitting image of Isla, but he was biased.

"Hello, Debra Prideaux," he whispered.

Debra didn't respond. She had just been fed, and she had no intention of waking up to impress anyone, not even her father. He studied the little girl keenly and touched her tiny fist, which was peeking out of the blanket. He saw a small black mark on the inside of her forearm, a birthmark the same as the cruel man that had made her. But, more importantly than that, he knew that Isla had told him the truth.

"Do you know where Miss Dickson is?" Mother Superior asked Brae.

He didn't take his eyes off Debra.

"Yes, I do, Mother. She has a few things to conclude. She will be home soon."

*

Artie couldn't rid himself of his temper. He slammed the door of the confessional. The priest had been dozing, and he awoke with a start.

"What on earth is the matter, Artie?" asked the man behind the screen. "You almost scared me to death," he accused.

The two had become good friends over the last months and even addressed each other on a first-name basis.

"James, I am so bloody furious. Isla has come home without the baby. She just left it at a convent somewhere in Falmouth. Can you try and find it? Surely, the nuns are caring for her?"

"Artie, calm down. If Isla had the child in the nursing home at the convent, we would certainly find the infant there. She is in the best care. Let me see what I can find out. I will let you know."

Artie's temper had not dissipated, and he slammed the door as he left the confessional. Father James restrained the impulse to judge Artie's behaviour. He knew that the kind, cheerful man must be at the end of his tether to behave that badly.

Artie rushed home, eager to confront Isla again. He crashed into the room he called home in a fit of temper, but it was empty. Isla was gone.

*

Two weeks later, Father James visited Artie.

"My friend, I have news of your granddaughter," he smiled at Artie.

"Granddaughter?" Artie laughed delightedly.

"Yes, a girl."

"Can I go and fetch her?" Artie's eyes were large with excitement.

"Unfortunately, not."

Artie's whole face dropped.

"Wait now, Artie," the Father told him. "A man named Brae Prideaux arrived at the convent two days after she was born claiming to be her father."

"Impossible," declared Artie, "completely impossible. We all know the truth. Dr Jennings will verify what I am saying."

"Brae Prideaux is the lighthouse keeper across from Falmouth. The man is well respected. We believe that Isla was working for him as a maid, he was deeply moved by the circumstances of your daughter, and he has declared himself the paternal parent."

"But why would he do that? Why would he take responsibility for another man's child?"

"There is only one explanation, Artie. He must love your daughter very much. He is a good man."

21

LOST

Isla was lost. She wasn't physically lost, but she had strayed so far from the moral code that Artie had instilled in her, that she didn't know how to find her way back. How would she get back to the solid foundation of life that she had before she was brutally raped by the stranger?

Isla found work at a small inn close to Bodmin, far from Victoria House. Nobody knew her there, and she kept herself to one side, wary of getting close to anyone who would try to mind her business.

Her employers were friendly enough, and the other girls were a lot of fun. Isla would smile and laugh, but she never divulged anything of her past, and she didn't participate in anything social.

Christmas came and went. She followed the Ashwin Jones' trial in the newspaper. The Welshman was hanged at dawn on a cold winter's day, along with the Wagner brothers, but she did not know who they were. There was a photo in the newspaper of a policeman called Jeremy Stevens who had trapped them and exposed their evil smuggling ring. He had a surprising resemblance to Sid.

Another Christmas passed by. Slowly, Isla began to find peace. The horror of the attack began to recede into the background of her mind.

She began to think of the baby she had given birth to. Where was she? Was she safe and cared for? As the horror receded, she spent time thinking about Brae Prideaux. He had loved her. He would have saved her had she allowed it. She considered going to Falmouth and searching for both of them. The child would be at the priory, orphanage or workhouse. The thought left Isla feeling despicable. Brae was at the lighthouse. He would never want her back. She had disappointed him when she gave up the baby. She must have disgusted him.

Night after night, the same thoughts ran through her mind. She couldn't rid herself of the compulsion to return to Falmouth. Just when she thought she was brave enough to go there, she lost her courage and changed her mind.

Yet another Christmas came and went. Isla had developed deep regrets. The rapist had ruined her life, but now she had ruined the lives of more than one person. She had outperformed her attacker. Her child, and innocent in the complexity of abuse. Her father, Artie Dickson, who had sacrificed everything for her, even his family farm. Was this the way to repay him after a lifelong investment of love?

Brae had been prepared to look after her. He was strong, kind and loyal. He would have been her friend for the rest of their lives. He was disappointed with her character. He would never forsake his own.

*

On her day off, Isla walked to Bodmin. She went to the train station and read the timetable, noting the time that the train from Bodmin ran to Devon. She needed to move away from Cornwall. She was too close to her past. She wanted to outrun it.

As she stood reading, her eyes kept darting down the page. Bodmin to Falmouth, Bodmin to Falmouth, Bodmin to Falmouth. Isla stood at the ticket counter, determined to get to Devon.

"Where to Miss?" asked the clerk.

Isla stalled.

"Where to, Miss?" The clerk insisted.

"Bodmin to Falmouth," she blurted.

The clerk shook his head. Who stood at a ticket counter if they didn't know where they were going?

"Thank you," said Isla. She looked down at the ticket, Bodmin to Falmouth.

*

Isla made her way back to the inn. She kept to the main road. She would never take a shortcut again, even if it cost her twenty miles. It was late evening, and the summer sun was persistent, and a storm was brewing over the moor.

Isla heard the sound of hooves behind her, but she felt no fear. She had experienced and survived the most severe, dehumanising violence. Nothing could intimidate her anymore.

She stepped to the side of the path, but the horse didn't pass her. She continued for a few seconds and swung around abruptly to see who it was.

The unsuspecting horse reared in fright, and the rider struggled to get it under control. She looked up and saw a cruel, smirking face. It was Peter Belmont. He was staring down at her, predatory and threatening.

He was taken aback by the woman's boldness. He would have preferred if she ran, but she looked up at him defiantly. He recognised Isla. He had seen her somewhere before. A strawberry-blonde lock hung out from under her hat, and she was beautiful. It suddenly dawned on Peter Belmont where he had seen her before. She had been a maid at Victoria Manor.

Isla was still beautiful but more mature. Her eyes were no longer the wide, terrified orbs that had aroused him. They were now narrowed, scathing and fearless.

"I know you," Peter Belmont drawled, "we have met before."

Isla met his gaze and stared at him until he looked away.

"Yes, we have," she said matter of fact.

"You were just a young thing then."

Peter Belmont dismounted the horse and walked towards her, but Isla didn't give way. Her boldness unsettled him.

Regardless, he put out his hand to touch her hair. Isla jerked her head back and caught his hand, and as she held it mid-air, she saw the birthmark on his wrist.

"You have become brave," he cooed as he had on the day he trapped her in the servant's corridor on the weekend of the hunt.

"You must be surprised to see my ghost," she taunted him, "you left me for dead in the woods. You trapped me in the copse on the Sunday of the hunt. You cowardly swine."

Peter stepped back. Being confronted for fiddling with a girl here and there was one thing. Attempted murder was another.

"No, I didn't," he objected loudly.

"Yes, you did. I recognised the birthmark on your wrist. And, I also survived to have your child."

Peter Belmont looked at her, not quite understanding what she was telling him.

"It has the same mark on its wrist."

"It's not mine, I swear. It wasn't me. I was nowhere close to Victoria Manor that Sunday night. Is it a boy?"

"I don't know. I gave it away."

Peter Belmont's mind was frantic. If the child was a boy and could be identified as a Belmont by the mark on its wrist, his whole inheritance could be at stake.

"I promise it is not mine. I left on the train early on Sunday morning. My father and I had an altercation, and I was not inclined to spend the weekend in his company. I made up an excuse and took the train from St Ives back to Oxford with my friends."

"Your friends are of poor character. They are not credible witnesses."

"My professors are, I attended my classes early on Monday morning,"

"Then why did the child have the same birthmark as you?"

Peter Belmont cast his mind back. He recalled his father warning him off the young maid. His father was adamant that she wasn't to be touched. She was the very cause of the upset.

"It's a family trait. My father has one on his wrist, as did my great-grandfather."

"And the latter of the two impregnated me from the grave," she sneered.

Peter searched her face, bewildered. His father had been reckless and deceiving. He knew that Peter wanted the girl, and that was why he warned him away. Which caring father would do that to his son? The man was a traitor. Peter Belmont had no further business with Isla. His business was with his father.

*

The sun had set over the moors, and Isla walked unhurriedly back to the inn. The knowledge meant nothing to her. Both men were abominable, like father, like son. She had no fear of Peter Belmont returning. All he could do was murder her, and be sure, there were many a day that she wished the attacker had.

The inn was peaceful, and she climbed the narrow staircase to the small room under the thatch. In the lamplight, she read the ticket again. Bodmin to Falmouth, one week away at noon. There was no excitement, only trepidation. She wasn't entitled to a second chance.

*

In the light of the full moon, Peter Belmont raced across the moor, determined to reach Victoria Manor as fast as he could. The horse was moving at full gallop. Isla's child was a threat to the family's good standing and his claim on the estate. They had to find it. After a hard ride, a relieved Peter could finally see Victoria Manor nestled in its beautiful grounds.

Peter Belmont stormed into the house, banging, slamming and screaming through the property until he reached his father's bedroom, where he crashed through the door unannounced.

Lord Belmont was sitting in the light of a gentle fire, smoking a cigar and looking at the pictures of the latest pornographic magazine from London.

"You are disgusting, you old swine," Peter screamed at his father.

His father looked up at him, alarmed.

"Get out of my bedroom. How dare you talk to me like this? What are you screaming about?"

"No. You listen to me, Father. Isla, the young maidservant you attacked and left for dead in the woods many years ago, is alive. I spoke to her. She lived. You should have killed her."

"What is the meaning of this attack, Peter?"

"Congratulations, Lord Belmont," he spat at his father in fury. "You are the father of a bastard, and you cannot disclaim it. It has a birthmark on its wrist, the mark of the Belmonts."

"Impossible," whispered Lord Belmont in disbelief. "Impossible."

"See for yourself."

"Go fetch the girl Peter, bring her back here. This can destroy the family."

"I will send somebody to get her," said Peter, "I am too tired to go back out on the moors."

"Balderdash! I am ordering you to fetch her, and you will leave right now. Your inheritance depends upon it."

*

Peter could cut three miles off his journey if he took a detour along a scruffy narrow path used by hunters. The horse was dripping with perspiration and becoming tired. The animal became unsettled when he steered it onto the hunting path. He had never travelled that way before, and it was dark. Peter expected the horse to retain its pace on the foreign path, which increased its anxiety.

At full gallop and highly stressed, the stallion saw a low rock ahead. Peter Belmont drove the animal harder, expecting it to jump, but it didn't. It stopped just short of the object. Its rider was propelled forward at the same speed and force as the horse in full gallop. He flew out of the stirrups and landed yards ahead of the powerful beast.

Belmont landed on the Cornish earth, hearing the crunch of the vertebrae close to his ears, amplified by bones of his skull. He died instantly and lay on the magnificent moor, a small insignificant heap. The horse was at peace, drinking from a watering hole, foraging in the succulent green grass.

*

Peter's death was not a soul-crushing blow to his father. The old man had never really liked his son, as often happened when people were too similar in character.

Lord Belmont paced his room. He had little choice but to make the long journey to the outskirts of Bodmin and consult the mad old witch who lived on a small tract of land. He had been there often. Her knowledge and skills were boundless. She had forewarned him on many issues.

*

He opened the yard gate and led his horse through the same debris that had littered it for the last ten years. He received no respect from Freya Dickson. She didn't open the gate for him, greet him, or offer him a drink. She would point to the red curtain, and the large ruby on her forefinger would flash in the firelight, like a lighthouse guiding him towards the dark of the séance room.

Freya didn't need any special powers to guess the state he was in.

"You have heard terrible news recently," she muttered, "your soul is in turmoil, perhaps a death in the family? I see a horse, a body slumped on the moor. Oh no!" Freya screamed dramatically, "I see your son. He cannot move. His neck is broken. And he's—dead!"

One of Freya's other patrons had told her the news, but Lord Belmont was impressed.

"Yes, yes, that is true, but it is not what is troubling me."

Freya laid out the tarot cards in front of them.

"Choose," Freya instructed.

Lord Belmont reached for the card, with the dark image of death holding the sickle.

"Clearly, the spirits are perplexed by your son's death. What more do you want to learn from them?"

"My son saw an apparition before he died. It was a person whom I killed many years ago."

"She is seeking redemption," whispered Freya.

"Can she kill me?"

"She cannot kill you, but she can lead you to death."

"How, how can she do that?"

"She will lead your mind astray and influence your choices. You will need a lot of wisdom."

Lord Belmont began to tell Freya the story, but she stopped him after a few words.

"I do not want to hear your dreary tale," but of course, Freya wanted to, yet sometimes denying somebody the right to speak made them more determined to tell the story, and Freya wanted every sordid detail.

"But how can you help me if I can't tell you what happened?" He asked anxiously.

"The spirit must speak for itself."

Freya lit a small bushel in a jar, and the room filled with a cloud of aromatic white smoke.

"The smell will put the spirit at ease, especially if it is malevolent."

Lord Belmont nodded.

Freya held his hands, and they closed their eyes. There were a frustrated few minutes while Freya tried to entice the spirit to cross over the chasm of death back to earth.

"I need a name. Who was this person?"

"I think her name was Dickson, Isla Dickson. She was just a servant girl, beautiful, but I couldn't bear the thought of sharing her. I had to kill her."

Freya was alert. She had not thought of Artie or Isla since they left the farm. She didn't care to remember them either.

"I need to know what she looked like so that I can recognise her."

Lord Belmont explained Isla in detail. He told Freya about the night in the woods. He shared every deep, dark, sick deed that he had enacted on her. Then he went on to say how much the maid had enjoyed it, but he wanted to keep it pure. Now, his son had seen her on the moor, and she had spawned a child.

"I want to know where that child is," he demanded of Freya.

"This will take time," whispered Freya dramatically. "You must be patient."

Freya had bought herself some time to think. She was attached to no one and nothing, yet she knew that he was talking about her daughter Isla. She had no depth of feeling for the girl, but she was incensed that Lord Belmont would put the same cruelty upon somebody else as her brothers had done on her. Her actions were entirely based upon her experiences in the past.

The room was filled with thick white smoke. Lord Belmont's eyes were closed, and she dropped a few leaves into the jar. The smell changed and became rancid and sweet like a rotting corpse.

"She is here," said Freya as if in a trance. "Can you see her?"

Lord Belmont opened his eyes and looked around.

"No, I can't, neither can I hear her."

"I can hear something screeching, screeching for mercy."

Lord Belmont's eyes shot open, terrified.

"Oh, no! This is grave. I cannot tell you this. You will never withstand it."

"What?" demanded Lord Belmont, "what? Tell me immediately."

Freya paused, and Lord Belmont became tense.

"She says she has killed your son, and she, with all the demons of hell, are coming to find you."

"What else?"

"She is gone. We were lucky she arrived at all."

*

Lord Belmont stood in the kitchen. He was pale as death itself. He was drenched in perspiration and overwhelmed by fear.

"Can you protect me?" He begged Freya.

"It is a complex spell. It will cost a lot of money."

"I will pay anything."

Freya smiled from ear to ear. There was nothing more powerful than death. People would pay anything to remain alive.

She put the thick treacly drops into the bottle, careful not to get them on her fingers.

"Four drops before you sleep, it will purify your dreams, enter your blood, nothing and nobody will touch you again, and you will suffer no more torment."

Freya was hoping he would suffer endless torment as he paid her handsomely.

*

Lord Belmont stopped at a small inn on the moors, just outside of Bodmin. The earlier he got to bed, the earlier he could take the mixture and have the fear and trepidation leave him.

"You will have to be patient," said the innkeeper, "one of our young maids left today for Falmouth. We are short-staffed."

Lord Belmont didn't undress. He was tired and frantic. He had to regain control, and Freya's spell would do that for him. He put four drops of the thick, bitter liquid onto his tongue. He felt his chest restrict, and he gasped for breath. He began to bring up blood and chunks of his stomach. He choked and wretched at the same time. Within a few minutes, he was dead.

The Falmouth Times published a large article on the front page, reporting the tragedy of son and father dying in the same week. More importantly, who would be the heir to their fortune.

22

REDEMPTION

Isla looked at the nun, her eyes were pleading for help, and Sister Bernadette felt sorry for her.

"She has been adopted," said the nun.

"By whom?" asked Isla.

"I can give you the dates, but not the name of the person who has taken her."

Isla wanted to weep with disappointment, but she chastised herself. She had no right to.

Sister Bernadette was away for some time, and Isla sat on a bare wooden bench, waiting for her.

Isla heard the click, click of boots approaching the office, and a heavy-set woman came inside and introduced herself as the Mother superior.

"Good day, Miss Dickson," said the Mother.

Isla greeted her.

"This situation is a strange one," she told Isla, "the man who adopted the child leaves a letter for you at the beginning of every year."

"A man?"

"Yes."

"It is also noted in our records that you are welcome to meet the little girl when you are ready to."

"Here," she passed the most recent letter to Isla.

Isla sat down on the bench and opened it.

Dear Isla

I have always had faith that you would return to us. You just needed time to take care of a few things. Debra, Artie, and I all live together at the lighthouse. For us, never a day goes by without thinking about you. I draw pictures of you for Debra so that she will know who her mummy is when she sees you. The ferry leaves Falmouth at noon. I have looked to see if you have been on it every day since you left.

I love you.

Brae

She folded the letter and saw something else in the envelope. She shook it, and something fluttered to the floor. She picked it up. It was a ferry ticket, valid for the whole year.

*

The ferry docked at the small wharf. She saw the stairs that she would need to climb to reach the lighthouse. She was so nervous that she stood on the wharf for some time. By three o'clock, she was still on the wharf. She wanted to return to Sherry at 'The Joe,' but she also clutched the letter.

The Ferryman yelled at her to get on or stay behind. She couldn't move. She couldn't speak. Eventually, he shook his head, started the large steam motors and left back to Falmouth.

*

Brae watched the person climbing the path towards him. It was very late. As the person got closer, he saw that it was a woman, and she was carrying a suitcase. Brae was too scared to wish, yet at the same time, he knew that it was Isla. He didn't have to see her face. It was an absolute in his mind that couldn't be shaken.

Brae started running down the path towards her. He was beside himself with joy and smiled from ear to ear. He reached her and flung his arms around her, and he heard her laugh. It was a symphony.

Then she remembered where she was, and her head dropped in shame. She couldn't meet his eyes.

His tanned rugged face looked down at her, he was as handsome as she remembered, and his eyes were ablaze with delight.

"Look at me," he told her fiercely.

She lifted her head, and he studied her. He took her face in his hands, tilted it, and kissed her.

He grabbed her suitcase in one hand and her hand in the other.

"Stop, stop." She called out.

He stopped.

"I am afraid, I am ashamed."

"Debra is expecting you."

Isla wanted to run, but Brae was firm, and he wouldn't let her go.

*

They reached a lawn, and she saw a little girl with a fizz of white hair around her face. Her eyes were large and round and happy.

Brae put his arm around Isla, pinning her to him.

"Don't be afraid of her, Isla. Look how precious she is."

Isla looked at the beautiful child.

"Look at that joy Isla, she is just like you. She has your smile and wild hair," he laughed, "and she is kind and loyal."

The little girl saw them and began to run towards her, Artie in tow.

"Mummy, mummy!" she yelled.

"She knows who I am," whispered Isla.

The little girl flung herself at her mother, and Isla picked her up.

"Are you better, Mama? Did you fix everything that you needed to?"

"Yes," said Isla, not daring to say any more.

Debra looked at Brae with adoration, then she touched Isla's hair.

"It's like my hair, Papa," Debra exclaimed.

"Yes, I told you it was," laughed Brae.

Debra touched Isla's face, ran her fingers down her mother's nose, and moved her hair out of the way to look at her ears. She left her mother's eyes for last. Isla couldn't help but smile during the inspection.

"Papa, she is just as you told me," said the little girl.

"How so?" said Brae, smiling.

Brae pulled Isla closer. These were the two loves of his life.

"She is very beautiful," gushed the girl.

"Oh, thank you," giggled Isla. "What else did Papa say about me?"

"Can I tell her, Papa?"

"Of course, you can, sweetheart," Brae smiled.

"My Papa said that you and I have the same eyes," she said solemnly.

"What else did I say?" asked Brae.

"You tell her Papa, you tell her!"

Brae couldn't hide his feelings any longer and stared down at her beautiful face and soft eyes.

"I told her that you have the most beautiful eyes, and one day when she looks into them, she will know why I love you."

*

Isla stood with her child in her arms, the man she loved held her close to his chest, and her father was running towards her, shouting welcomes and making a lot of noise.

Isla was happy. She had made her way home.

—————

Like The Lighthouse Keeper's Lass? Here are some more books in my 'Victorian Village Scandals' series you'll love. Have you read them all?

The Widow of the Valley

1880s Wales. After marrying for love, Derryn Morgan flees Cardiff's slums for the tranquil valleys. Moving into a cosy cottage with a handsome man by her side, life seemed perfect. But the heartbreaking whine of the mine's dreadful siren snuffed all that out in an instant. Rather than being supported by the community, penniless, she is ostracised.

Worse, she discovers a terrible secret about her beloved husband. Everything she holds dear is torn away. Will she always be struggling, alone and unloved, or, by using all her inner resolve is there hope for a better future?

- https://mybook.to/ValleyWidow

The Urchin of Walton Hall

England, 1865. A young lovechild is abandoned by her sickly and desperate mother at Walton Hall. Swiftly, she is sent away by her philandering father to escape his vengeful wife's disdain. Alas, a tragic near-fatal accident strikes her papa, and the decline of the family's fortunes means they face destitution. After a series of failed encounters with suitors, her stepmother takes drastic measures against the unwanted lass. Who is the mystery fiancé she has in mind to finally free her of the shameful stepchild that ruined her life? And how will Bess feel knowing her betrothal means she will never be free to marry her childhood sweetheart?

- https://mybook.to/EHUrchin

... or scan here to view the series on Amazon.

GET THREE FREE AND EXCLUSIVE EMMA HARDWICK OFFERS

Hi! Emma here. For me, the most rewarding thing about writing books is building a relationship with my readers and it's a true pleasure to share my experiences with you. From time to time, I write little newsletters with short snippets I discover as I research my Victorian historical romances, details that don't make it into my books. In addition, I also talk about how writing my next release is progressing, plus news about special reader offers and competitions.

And I'll include all these freebies if you join my newsletter:

- A copy of my introductory novella, The Pit Lad's Mother.
- A copy of my introductory short story, The Photographer's Girl.
- A free copy of my Victorian curiosities, a collection of newspaper snippets I have collated over the years that have inspired many of the scenes in my books.

These are all exclusive to my mailing list—you can't get them anywhere else. You can grab your free books on BookFunnel, by signing up here:

- https://rebrand.ly/eh-free

ENJOYED THIS BOOK?
YOU CAN MAKE A BIG DIFFERENCE

Reviews are the most powerful tools in my arsenal when it comes to getting attention for my books. Much as I'd like to, I don't have the financial muscle of a New York publisher. I can't take out full page ads in the newspaper or put posters on the subway, or appear on a prime time chat show.

(Not yet, anyway).

But I do have something much more powerful and effective than that, and it's something that those publishers would kill to get their hands on - avid readers who are loyal and supportive.

Honest reviews of my books help bring them to the attention of others who will enjoy them. If you've got something to share about this book I would be very grateful if you could spend just a minute or two leaving a review (it can be as short as you like) on the book's Amazon page.

I really appreciate your feedback. It helps me improve my books.

If you'd like be a member of my 'Book Squad' and be an advance reviewer of my books before they are launched, you can find out more on the next page.

CAN YOU HELP ME WITH MY NEXT BOOK?

Like the chance to read my stuff before it hits Amazon? Read on.

One of the best things I did last year was set up Emma's 'Book Squad'. It is critically important to get reviews on new books as soon as they launch. You probably weigh reviews highly when making a decision whether to try a new author or rely on an old favourite - I know that I do. Apart from helping to persuade people to give a new writer a shot, reviews help drive early sales which, in turn, means that Amazon takes notice and starts to tell more people about my books so more people can enjoy them.

To make that happen I have a small team of 'advance readers'. It's pretty simple and is, I hope, good fun. It involves them being sent a copy of whatever book I've just finished and then, when it is published, firing up a quick and honest review. Simple as that. Some members of the team have picked up errors that I've been able to correct and others have suggested changes to the plot that I have incorporated.

Apart from getting a copy of the latest book before anyone else, I try to say thanks with some exclusive competitions. In some circumstances, I offer signed print editions, else things like limited edition mugs. I try to keep the team relatively compact. There are a couple of vacancies at the moment and if you would like to get involved, please let me know. You can apply here: https://bit.ly/EH-ST

ABOUT THE AUTHOR

Emma Hardwick is the author of several series of Victorian historical saga romances. She lives in London with her husband, and dogs and makes her online home at:

- www.emmahardwick.co.uk

You can connect with Emma on Facebook at :
- www.facebook.com/emmahardwickauthor

and if the mood takes you, you should send her an email at:

- hello@emmahardwick.co.uk

ALSO BY EMMA HARDWICK

Here's a full set of all my historical romance series. You can view all my books on my on my Amazon page.

The Hudson Family Saga

Set in Victorian England, two heartrending tales of torment, struggle, and love that follow the Hudsons between 1849 up to the late 1890s. Join the heroines, determined to fight for their own independence and success, no matter what grave betrayals, hardships and catastrophes befall them.

See all books in the series

- https://rebrand.ly/HFSaga

The Victorian Runaway Girls

Join these tenacious Victorian women as they strive to break from their bleak past and bring true love into their future. Whether abandoned, forgotten, or mistreated, each of the women has a reason to flee and never return.

See all books in the series

- https://rebrand.ly/RGSaga

The Victorian Sisters Saga

Two sisters. Two very different lives. In the Victorian era, fate can be cruel or fate can be kind. Which sister will thrive and who will be doomed—and why?

See all books in the series

- https://rebrand.ly/SSSaga

The Victorian Sisters Saga

Two sisters. Two very different lives. In the Victorian era, fate can be cruel or fate can be kind. Which sister will thrive and who will be doomed—and why?

See all books in the series

- https://rebrand.ly/SSSaga

The Victorian Christmas Chronicles

Get into the festive spirit and join these vivacious, strong Victorian lasses fighting for a brighter future, despite many cruel obstacles in these feel-good tales of courage and determination, each with a wonderful yuletide backdrop.

See all books in the series

- https://rebrand.ly/CCSaga

Printed in Great Britain
by Amazon